Chin
and the
Magic Stones

Chin
and the
Magic Stones

BOOK ONE

BECOMING GUARDIANS

L.J. SALAZAR

iUniverse, Inc.
New York   Bloomington

Chin and the Magic Stones
Book One - Becoming Guardians

iUniverse books may be ordered through booksellers or by contacting:

iUniverse
1663 Liberty Drive
Bloomington, IN 47403
www.iuniverse.com
1-800-Authors (1-800-288-4677)

ISBN: 978-0-595-53157-8 (pbk)
ISBN: 978-0-595-63627-3 (cloth)
ISBN: 978-0-595-63219-0 (ebk)

Printed in the United States of America

iUniverse rev. date: 2/19/2009

For up-to-date information about Chin and the Magic Stones series, bulk
orders, special discounts for schools and libraries, or press inquiries, please visit
us on the Web at www.chinandthemagicstones.com.

For high-resolution posters of the illustrations included in this book, please
visit our Web site.

For Yolanda, Luis E, Super Abuelos, Ana, and Eagle

CHAPTER 1 ———

A Shiny Discovery

CHIN WAS TEN YEARS OLD AND lived in Kirkland, a small city that borders a big lake in Washington State.

He had a dog, a Cavalier King Charles Spaniel that his dad had brought home with him from a business trip to London. Chin often dreamed about flying and traveling to distant places, like his dad, where he'd have new adventures and fight great battles. Chin loved eagles, so he chose Eagle as the perfect name for his loyal dog.

Chin was also a stone collector and enjoyed reading adventure books. But as much as he loved adventures and fantasy tales, he never expected to be part of a real quest—a quest that would change his life forever.

Little did he know that he and his loyal dog, Eagle, would become the appointed guardians of a secret, the holders of nine magic stones, and the leaders of a magical revolution that unveiled formulas that only children could use. They would also become warriors in charge of facing a fantastical being known as the Shadow Lord who was protected by a court of loyal and creepy creatures.

One Sunday at the beginning of spring break, Chin was helping his dad with yard work. It was a sunny afternoon in late April, and the weather was perfect: cool and breezy with a nip in the air. The cold winter season had been particularly hard in the Pacific Northwest that year.

Chin was cleaning up mud and debris from some rocks he found around the pond in the garden when he came across one stone that was shining more than any other.

The stone was roughly the size of a twenty-five cent coin and was thin and flat in the shape of an arrowhead. It was warmer than the others too, even though it was in a shaded corner of the garden, behind a big cedar tree and partially submerged in the pond.

It was not the burning-sizzling-blistering kind of hot like Chin often described hot things, but it was warm. When holding the rock steady in his hand, he could even feel some shaking—a buzz or vibration similar to feeling a trapped insect trying to fly away from a closed hand.

"Dad! Look at this stone," Chin exclaimed. "I think it's from a volcano because it's still warm and it's kind of shiny."

"Hmm, let me take a closer look," Dad replied. "Well, yes, it's beautiful and looks very special, but it doesn't seem that warm or shiny to me. Maybe you saw the stone reflecting the sunlight? It could be a mix of some metallic particles. Maybe that's why it shines under the sunlight."

Chin was confused. He looked at the stone in his dad's hand—it was shining with a soft blue glow that was certainly not the sunlight reflected on the stone's surface.

Chin knew one or two things about rocks, and he was sure that subtle glow was not the result of light reflecting from the rock's surface. His dad was under the shadow of the big Japanese maple in their garden; no sunlight was directly reaching the stone, and yet Chin could see the smooth, blue glow.

"Maybe you're right, Dad," Chin said hesitantly. "Let me clean it up a bit more."

"Save it with your other rocks," Dad said. "Take it with you inside and check your books to see if you can learn something about it. I'd love to learn more about your discovery later. Maybe you can tell me more at dinnertime."

Chin agreed and ran into the house. Eagle ran by his side, jumping around and waving his tail, ready to play.

"Come on, Eagle," Chin said, petting his dog. "Let's go to my room and study this beautiful rock."

"Of course, Chin, let's go to your room. I really want to bite one of your teddy bears."

"No problem! You can play ... with ..." But Chin stopped in the middle of the staircase without finishing his sentence. He could not believe Eagle was speaking to him.

"It must be my imagination," said Chin aloud, talking to himself.

"What did you say, honey?" called his mom from the kitchen, where she was cooking dinner.

"Uh, nothing, Mom. Did you hear anything?"

"Why yes—I heard you calling the dog and Eagle barking and jumping. Do you need anything?" Mom added, coming to the foot of the stairs.

"No, Mom. Did you hear Eagle barking or, uh ... talking?"

"What do you mean?" asked his mom, chuckling.

3

"Nothing, Mom ... of course Eagle was just barking. You know sometimes I get confused with English and Spanish words."

Chin dashed up to his room, holding the rock tightly as Eagle jumped around him. He opened the window to let in the fresh air. He loved the smell of wet dirt and leaves that came from the garden every evening during these beautiful spring days.

Eagle sat down in a corner, carefully watching the teddy bears, but the aroma of spring from the garden distracted him. He started to sniff around with his head and nose up, moving around and breathing deeply at a fast pace.

Chin put the rock on his desk and grabbed his wooden box with his rock collection. He opened the box and tried to find a similar rock, but it was pointless; nothing was even close. He took his book about rocks and read page by page, comparing each picture and each description with his new discovery. He looked for an explanation for that mysterious glow.

Two hours passed and Eagle was sleeping across Chin's lap. Chin took a break from reading the book and contemplated Eagle resting peacefully. Eagle was a short and small dog, with a beautiful, thick brown and white coat, and very long and furry ears. As he was sleeping, his long whiskers moved in cadence with his nose, up and down. He was maybe dreaming about sniffing some good food. Even when sleeping, Eagle kept wagging his long tail as a signal of happiness.

Tired after the unsuccessful research, Chin took the rock in his hand. It was still warm and still glowing with that deep blue color and soft light, even inside his room and far from the window where the sunlight could not hit the rock's surface. It was still buzzing with its now-familiar tune.

"What kind of rock could this be?" Chin asked himself.

"I don't know its name, but I've seen that rock many times in the garden," said Eagle. "It's my favorite rock—when I'm playing in the garden I spend hours looking at it. I love the blue light, and my friend Seahawk loves to perch on top of that rock while talking to me."

"Eagle!" Chin replied in astonishment. "Do you understand me?"

"Of course," Eagle replied calmly. "But I didn't know that you could talk Doggy. Congratulations, because you do it very well."

"I do not speak Doggy," Chin insisted. "You speak English!"

Eagle laughed. "What do you mean, Chin? I cannot speak Human; I just know how to bark, and I love the way you talk to me in Doggy language. I think Doggy is one of the best languages in the world, because a dog in China can talk to an Italian dog or to a North American dog, and we all understand each other. That is why we do not have big fights among dog species, because we can easily understand each other. But you, the humans, sure know how to make things complex—you speak in too many languages."

Chin's hazel eyes always turned a bit greener when he got excited about something. His eyes were very green now as he listened to his dog talking. But he was confused; he could hear Eagle talking in perfect English, but his dog insisted they were talking Doggy language.

"Yes, I do congratulate you for learning how to speak Doggy," Eagle continued. "You do not even have any accent. If I close my eyes and listen to you, I cannot tell it is not a nice and well-educated dog talking to me, maybe a British dog from a nice London neighborhood."

Chin was beginning to feel annoyed. He was ten years old, he was a brave fifth grader, and he decided he was not going to let a two-year-old King Charles Cavalier dog make a fool of him, telling him he was speaking Doggy language.

Chin dropped the rock and asked Eagle to move away from his lap. Eagle jumped from Chin's lap and barked happily while chewing on one of Chin's old teddy bears.

Chin had a beautiful collection of stuffed toy animals that his dad and his grandpa had brought him from their many trips. Chin thought about all those toys from different parts of the world and about the many different languages spoken in those countries.

He had friends from Finland, India, Colombia, China, Venezuela, Italy, France, and Spain, yet he realized they always spoke in English in order to understand each other.

Chin suddenly realized it would be awesome to be able to speak to everybody—any people in the world, any animal, maybe even any toy or object.

He was sure that objects could tell many stories, maybe even ones about ancient battles! He was a bit aggravated with Eagle, but he knew Eagle was right about the convenience of sharing a common language among all humans.

Chin remembered when he was three years old and arrived in the United States with his family. He spoke Spanish very well but could not speak English and could not understand other kids, but somehow playing together was an international language, and he made new friends just by playing with them.

He also remembered his dad telling him that when he was three years old, he often roared like a little lion instead of talking. Pretending to be an animal was a common language among three-year-olds, and roaring was understood in Chinese, German, English, or any other language.

Chin could barely remember what it was like when he was three years old, but he was sure it worked every time, since the other kids very often started to roar and bark as well, pretending they were little animals while playing together.

"Eagle; don't bite that teddy bear, and please drop it. I'm not in the mood for playing," Chin snapped.

"Woof! Woof!" Eagle replied.

"Eagle, talk to me in English, please," Chin said fervently.

"Woof, woof, woof!" Eagle answered again.

"Eagle, tell me just one word, and I'll let you play with my new rock, the one you like so much," said Chin, grabbing his rock.

"Woof," Eagle repeated. "Certainly, Chin, but I can only speak Doggy."

Chin stared at the rock in his hand. He suddenly realized something remarkable: when he had grabbed the rock, he started to understand Eagle. Chin was a fast thinker and a good learner, and he had so many ideas swirling in his mind that brought many possible scenarios of fantasy and reality crashing together.

"What is this—a magic stone? I knew this stone was special— no wonder I couldn't find it in my rock books. No wonder it was shining even when it wasn't hit by sunlight. No wonder ... no wonder ..."

Chin put the rock in his pocket and jumped around, dancing with Eagle. In the distance he heard the sound of the bells ringing at Carillon Point, the old marina in Kirkland. Chin paid attention to the bells and counted them: one, two, three, four, five, six, and then silence.

"It's already six o'clock; no wonder I'm so hungry. Let's go and see what's for dinner, Eagle. But first, let's put the rock in a safe place. It could be a very precious stone, and I don't want to lose it or misplace it."

Chin looked for a safe place for his stone, but he couldn't find anything to match the perfect box he had pictured in his mind—a box fit to hold his magic stone.

Somehow, he had envisioned a small blue box with the silhouette of a colorful butterfly on the lid. His friend Forrest, a Native American chief of the Hopi tribe in Arizona, told him once that butterflies represented the cycle of life and joy.

Forrest had told Chin that every problem was a butterfly in disguise—that beyond the apparent problem, he could always find the shiny part, the butterfly. Chin did not understand it very well at the time, but Forrest told him not to worry because the meaning would find him when he was ready.

Since then, Chin looked differently at butterflies, always expecting a magic revelation, a secret formula to solve problems, anticipating mysterious secrets he was sure would come out of a butterfly.

Chin had a very clear image in his mind of the box he was looking for—he could see it and almost touch it with his hands if he focused enough.

He was convinced that the box existed somewhere and that by painting a clear picture in his mind, he would be able to find it at the right time.

Chin did not know that by visualizing that box, some magical forces of the universe were set in motion. Little did he know that the box would appear in his life very soon.

CHAPTER 2

Chin Wants a Real Bow and Arrow

CHIN WENT TO BED THAT NIGHT thinking about the box he wanted for his magic stone. Visualizing things was kind of a pastime for Chin. His dad often encouraged him to stay quiet and meditate to build things in his mind.

When his dad first told him to practice, it wasn't easy for him to visualize, and he often found himself getting distracted and thinking about the fantasy book he was reading or about the play date he would have the next day. But the first time he manifested a real visualization, it was a magical moment and a milestone in developing his ability.

At the time, he was eight years old, and he was in Arizona with his mom and his dad. It was an autumn day and they had gone there to celebrate his parents' anniversary. They were excited about visiting the Grand Canyon, Sedona, and the Kartchner Caverns.

That day, Chin and his dad lay down on the grass by the hotel swimming pool and looked up at the sky. They loved to play a game of trying to vaporize the clouds by staring at them. Chin was always amazed at how his dad was always able to make clouds disappear in just seconds.

Chin simply pointed to one cloud, and before he could finish asking his dad to vaporize that cloud, he would see an empty piece of blue sky among the other clouds.

"Dad, can you please teach me your magic trick? I'm trying hard, but I can't move a cloud even a little bit!"

"Well," his dad answered, "how do you try to do it? What are you thinking about as you try?"

"That's easy—I think about a powerful laser beam, one even bigger than the Death Star's, one that can vaporize planets. Then I focus all the power of that laser beam on the cloud that I want to make disappear."

"Hmm, that sounds like too much, but it should work," Dad said, chuckling as he imagined that big laser beam pointing at the defenseless cloud.

"But it hasn't worked yet. I haven't tried a lot; so I'm not sure if it's gonna work. So far it hasn't," Chin said with disappointment.

"Chin, you will often get what you expect. If you are fearful, you will often get fearful results; if you have doubts, you can get doubts back. Why do you think you so easily learned how to ride a bike? Or how to speak a different language? Those were new things!"

"Dad, riding a bike was easy, and learning a new language is super easy for me. But vaporizing clouds is not!"

"Close your eyes and just imagine the cloud is not there anymore," Dad said calmly. "Just picture in your mind a perfect piece of empty, clean sky, nothing else. Just imagine that—no lasers, no powerful weapons, just relax. Do not think 'no cloud,' because if you think of disappearing the cloud, you are still focused on the cloud, thus making it too big in your mind rather than smaller."

Chin closed his eyes, relaxed, and forgot about using powerful rays or complex machines. He just thought about a perfect piece of blue and orange sky to match the colors of that beautiful sunset in the Arizona desert.

He thought it would be funny to see a perfect square drawn in the cloud; he imagined how people would react to such a thing in the sky; he could almost hear the comments from the hotel guests, the employees, all pointing to the sky and marveling at that perfect and unusual square.

"Good job," his dad said suddenly. "I like the square—very creative."

Chin opened his eyes and saw a perfect square of blue and orange sky in the middle of a heavy white cloud.

"But, Dad, I didn't do anything! I was just having fun imagining a square; I wasn't even trying—"

"But you did it!" Dad said, putting his arm around Chin.

Chin was afraid and confused. How he could possibly make such a thing happen? he wondered. Was that magic? In any case, he was proud of himself and decided to take advantage of whatever had really happened.

"Since I'm such a good apprentice, can I get something as a reward? I want a real bow and arrow, not a toy one, not one made out of plastic. I want the real thing!"

"Good, then work on it!" said his dad, chuckling.

"No, Dad, no tricks, I really want a real bow and arrow."

"Chin, you just vaporized a perfect square inside a humongous white cloud that was more than one thousand feet away from us, and you don't believe you can get a bow and arrow?"

"Oh, Dad, yes I can get it, I can imagine it, and I see you giving it to me!" said Chin cheerfully.

"Well, that is certainly a way. It could also happen that you win it in a contest, or you could find a way to make some extra money and buy it at a store. It could happen in so many ways. Close your eyes and imagine you are getting the bow and arrow. I am sure it will come your way," Dad added.

It was a beautiful sunset in Arizona, and the sky was burning orange and red. His dad went back to their room to get ready for dinner.

Chin stayed outside, looking at the sky, but he was not vaporizing clouds anymore. He was thinking about a beautiful bow and arrow, imagining his hands holding it and getting ready for many battles...

Later that night, they were on their way out of the hotel to have dinner at an Italian restaurant nearby. Chin's mom stopped at a display of Native American artifacts. It was a small exhibition in the lobby of the hotel. Chin was excited to see real bows and arrows used by Native American tribes when hunting for food.

He created in his mind scenes of battles and hunting trips. Suddenly he was interrupted by an old man who approached them and asked, "Do you like that one? My tribe made those. The small ones are for training our kids when they are four years old, the medium ones are for our little warriors when they are nine years old—with those they can start hunting small birds."

The old man's name was Forrest and he was the chief of the Hopi tribe in Arizona; he told Chin about the many Hopi legends and stories, and Chin was fascinated listening to him and examining the beautiful artifacts.

Chin looked at Forrest's face as Forrest spoke. It was covered by many lines and wrinkles and had a very healthy color, a bit red, like everything else in Arizona. Chin noticed that everything in Arizona had that beautiful reddish tone that glowed even brighter when hit by the sunlight. Forrest was maybe seventy years old, because he looked a lot like Chin's grandpa that was also seventy years old. But instead of being a bit bald like grandpa, Forrest had very long and mostly gray hair that was tied in a ponytail. Chin heard Forrest talking, but he was fascinated and almost distracted by Forrest's purple eyes, dark and thick eyebrows and by the commanding presence of the old chief.

"Do you want me to make a real one for you?" asked Forrest for a third time, with a soft but firm voice that brought Chin back to the conversation. "It will take me just four days. But I would do so only if your parents agree, of course."

"Do you mean a real bow and arrow?" asked Chin in surprise, barely containing his excitement and looking at his parents, begging for permission.

"Of course I will make a real one," said Forrest. "I shall go to the mountain tonight and get the wood from the branch of a strong, ancient tree. Tonight will be a full moon, and I like to go out way beyond the desert, up to the mountains. When I do that, I can hear my ancestors talking to me about the magic and secrets of our tribe. They tell me how we need to keep our old secrets alive and transmitted from one generation to the next. If your parents give permission, I can make a very special bow and arrows for you."

"Can I have it, Dad?" cried Chin, excited by the prospect.

"Of course you can, Chin; you created it in your mind, so you deserve it," added his dad proudly.

"I see," said Forrest. "Is this young man already manifesting things? Let me look at your eyes, son."

Forrest looked into Chin's eyes, which made Chin a bit uncomfortable.

"You are right," said Forrest seriously. "I can see clearly that this young man is a good apprentice; I will make a special bow with seven silver arrows. It will take me longer, because I need to walk to the top of the Red Rocks in Sedona and take the silver wood out of the west cavern. But it must be done that way."

Chin and his parents did not understand Forrest's words, but it was a magic moment for Chin. He realized how powerful visualization could be and began to see how to attract things into his life by being positive and thinking about them.

"Dad, this whole thing about visualizing, imagining … Is some sort of magic or just coincidences happening?"

"That is for you to figure it out," said his dad, chuckling.

It was the beginning of a journey, and Chin did not realize at that time the many quests he would experience or the perils he would face in the future. The adventure was just starting, and his bow and arrow would play a crucial role in his future journeys.

Chin relaxed on his bed, remembering these episodes from last fall.

"Everything is starting to make sense; I think I am ready," whispered Chin, just before falling asleep.

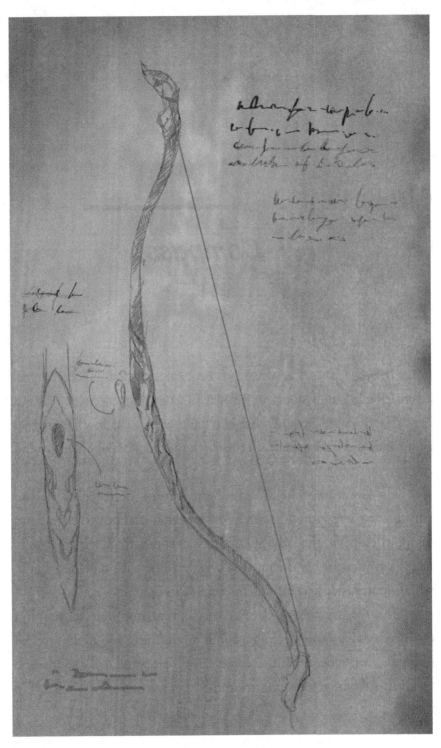

CHAPTER 3 ━━━━━━

A Compass

CHIN DREAMT ABOUT A PLACE WITH people, animals, and creatures all wearing brilliant stones in necklaces, rings, and earrings. It was a happy dream, but he could sense a cold presence, a shadow wearing no gemstones and hiding beneath the earth in some sort of underground caverns.

He saw how somehow the light coming out of each person and creature was vibrating at a high frequency and how the shadows disappeared when the light of hundreds of stones filled the emptiness of the caverns. In his dream was a giant door with a golden knob, which spun faster and faster, counterclockwise.

The stones in the necklaces, rings, and earrings were all spinning counterclockwise too, finding a common rhythm. Still dreaming, he saw rain everywhere. Multicolored raindrops painted the landscape as Chin suddenly felt a warm and wet sensation on his face. He started to laugh when he realized it was Eagle licking his face to wake him up.

"Eagle, stop it! I'm already awake!"

But Eagle kept licking Chin's face, wanting to be sure Chin was alert and ready for the day's adventures.

"Woof, woof!" Eagle barked, looking at the magic stone that Chin had put on his desk next to his bed.

"Okay, Eagle, I get it; you want to talk to me. Let me grab the stone."

Chin grabbed the stone; he was pleased to feel the now-familiar warm, smooth surface of the magic stone.

"Let's go Chin!" Eagle barked, jumping around. "Hurry up— it's already past seven and we have to get to Carillon Point before nine o'clock or we'll have to wait for another day."

"What for, Eagle?" Chin asked.

"My friend, Seahawk, told me to get to the clock at Carillon Point before nine o'clock and to stand at the end of the shadow cast by the third column. Just when we hear the ninth ring from the bells, we must put the stone on the floor at the end of the shadow with the stone's pointy side facing north. Hurry up, we don't have much time!"

Chin was still sleepy and couldn't understand everything that Eagle said, but he jumped out of bed and went to the bathroom to wash his face, brush his teeth, and get ready for the trip to Carillon Point.

While brushing his teeth, he thought about how to figure out if the stone was pointing north; he realized he needed a compass, but he didn't have one.

"I need a compass," he told Eagle. "I need one I can carry with me."

He saw the compass in his mind; he could see himself holding it and finding north.

"Chin, breakfast is ready," his mom called upstairs to him. "Please come down and bring Eagle with you. And please bring your dad's briefcase that's on top of his desk."

Chin got dressed in his black shorts with the USA flag printed on both sides, his yellow shirt with the Brazilian National Soccer team logo, and his black jacket with the Canadian National Hockey team logo. He was truly a representative of the *worldwide citizenship order*—a term his father used often to describe how people should think about themselves: as habitants of mother earth, with no boundaries among countries.

He opened his top bureau drawer where he kept all his hats. He had a collection of hats from every Major League Baseball team, which his grandpa had given to him. He also had hats from football teams, soccer teams, countries, capital cities, states, and even movies.

He chose his favorite black hat, put the magic stone in his pocket, and walked downstairs as Eagle raced down by his side.

"Honey, are you bringing your dad's briefcase with you?" his mom called upstairs.

"Of course, Mom," Chin answered, chuckling to himself as he raced back upstairs to grab the forgotten briefcase. "I always remember to do what you tell me."

"Mom, I'm ready," added Chin while taking his place at the breakfast table. "Good morning, Dad; here's your briefcase."

"Thanks, Chin. I wanted to give you a little present—it's a small survival kit I got from a travel magazine I'm doing some photographic work for. It comes with a compass, a whistle, protein energy bars, and a water cooler. I think you'll enjoy it during spring break when you explore the woods with your friends."

"Thanks, Dad!" Chin exclaimed. "It's just what I needed today—a compass!" Chin hugged his dad.

"You can always get what you really need and want," said his dad. "It's just a matter of—"

"Visualizing it and being positive," said Mom, Chin, and even Eagle at the same time. They were used to Chin's dad's speech.

"Where are you going this morning, son? Do you need a ride?"

"Actually I do, Dad. Can you please take us to Carillon Point? It's close by, but I have to be there before nine o'clock. I'll go with Eagle, and I'm taking the short-wave radio with me in case I need to talk to Mom."

Chin pulled the radio out of his jacket pocket and flipped the switch. "Testing, one, two, three," said Chin while holding his black radio close to his mouth. "Can you hear me, Mom?"

"Loud and clear. Over," said Mom, signing off.

"So, Chin, what is going on at Carillon Point at nine o'clock?" Dad asked.

"Well, the Seahawk told Eagle to go there and put the magic stone on the floor at the end of the shadow that the third column casts at exactly that time," Chin said enthusiastically.

"Oh, I see," Mom said, chuckling. "I love how you play with your imagination, Chin."

Chin didn't have time to explain the exciting developments of the last twenty-four hours, and he decided he would share details with his parents at dinnertime. Now he was focused on getting to Carillon Point.

"We're ready, Chin," Dad said. "Please take Eagle's harness and your bag with your compass, energy bar, and bottled water, and wait for me."

In the garage, Chin was excited about the adventure awaiting him at the marina. He knew that everything was going to be perfect.

Chin was a joyful boy and had been taught by his parents to trust his feelings and to embrace life with a positive outlook. It worked both ways; when he was doubtful or afraid, the results were not good—his fears often affected results. When he embraced new adventures with a positive visualization of the outcome, he often found great joy in the journey and a rewarding experience.

He was thinking about this while unplugging their electric car from the power outlet. He read the power meter and saw that it was 90 percent charged. That charge was more than enough for his trip to Carillon Point and for his dad's commute to work at his photography studio in Lake Union.

"Dad, the car is ready—it is almost fully charged, and I've put the charging cable in the trunk, plus Eagle's harness, my compass, my radio, and my water bottle."

"Have a good day, son," said Mom. "Stay safe and call me when you want me to pick you up. I'll be running some errands and can give you and Eagle a ride back home after your adventures at the secret passage in the marina."

CHAPTER 4 ━━━━━━━

A Magic Door

IT WAS A SUNNY DAY, AND the marina was full of life, with people getting ready for trips in their boats. It was still early, and Chin had fifteen minutes before nine o'clock. He went to the end of the dock to watch the boats cruising the lake and the fishermen waiting patiently for a fish.

Chin stared at the seagulls trying to steal the bait from the fishermen's buckets, and he grabbed the stone from his right pocket to examine it under the sun's soft morning rays.

While examining the stone, he thought about the things he could learn from Eagle and how he could train Eagle to amaze his friends at school and in the neighborhood.

"That's a beautiful stone—where did you find it?" asked the old seagull that Chin had been staring at. The seagull seemed to have a European accent, possibly from Spain.

"What?" gasped Chin.

"He wants to know where you found the stone," said Eagle, laughing.

"But, Eagle, can you also talk to birds? And how come birds can talk too?" Chin asked.

"The stone!" said the seagull. "We can communicate with all the species when we are close to that type of stone. Didn't you learn that at school? I thought your teacher Mrs. Sallice knew about it, as I have seen her collecting stones. What do they teach at school these days?"

Chin was still confused; somehow it was easier to accept that the stone had magic powers for making him communicate with Eagle. But talking to a stranger like the old seagull was a different thing. And how did the seagull know about Mrs. Sallice? Everything felt confusing to him.

"Hurry up, boy," said the old seagull. "It's almost nine o'clock, and the bells will start ringing any minute now."

"How did you know about the bells? How do you know about the stone? What's your name? Can you understand me?"

Chin was almost whispering—he didn't want to look like a fool in front of the fishermen. But they were too busy fighting seagulls away from their bait.

"They call me Super Abuelo, which means *Super Grandpa* in Spanish, and you can call me that too. As to your other questions, we must have that conversation another day. You have to run now."

As Super Abuelo spoke, Chin heard the first chime of the bells. He had eight seconds to run to the old carillon and put the stone on the floor.

Chin ran fast, with Eagle by his side; his heart was pounding as he got closer to the carillon, and he was counting the rings: two, three; only a few more steps, four, five, six; he was right there, with the compass in one hand and the stone in the other; seven, eight, Eagle was pointing with his nose toward the end of the shadow of the third column. Chin looked for north on his compass and then put the stone on the floor in the perfect place, by the end of the shadow.

The last ring had a different sound; it was a long, dark and sustained pitch, like the sound of a giant Chinese gong. Chin was a bit dizzy, and he thought it was because of the sprint to get to the carillon on time.

His breathing was normal, but everything was spinning around; only Eagle by his side and the rock in the floor were in focus; everything else was distorted and tinted by a brilliant green and yellow light.

The shape of a door started to appear in the surface of the concrete floor, below the stone, and once it was completed, the rock was in the perfect place to serve as the knob of that strange door.

Chin turned the knob clockwise, but it was locked; he tried counterclockwise as he did in his dream last night. It worked—the door opened, and he saw stairs going down to an underground cave. Soft blue lights illuminated it, and Chin and Eagle heard the sound of water splashing coming from the bottom of the stairs.

"Move on, Chin," Eagle said impatiently. "I'm really thirsty, and I hear and smell water down there."

"Eagle, wait," Chin replied. "Let me grab my radio and try to get a flashlight …"

But it was too late—Eagle was already bounding downstairs. Chin grabbed the stone, and as soon as he entered the cellar behind Eagle, the door closed behind them. A glowing circle marked the place where the stone had been acting as a knob a few seconds ago.

His eyes slowly adapted to the dim light, and he found himself and Eagle in front of the third column of the carillon. But now each one of the six columns was several hundred feet tall and almost ten feet wide, in a cavern so big he could not see the roof—only the soothing blue lights floating in the air, surrounding them.

Each column had a gold and silver door that was almost five feet wide by almost twenty feet tall, guarded by marble statues of spearmen that were at least ten feet tall.

Each door had a unique design with a special encryption in dark letters: Creo, Cōnātus-Nitor, Dono, Seiunctus, Facultās, and Propositum. At the center of the semicircle, down in the floor, an additional word was engraved in dark brown letters: *Cognitio.* At the other end of the semicircular hall was a small water fountain.

"Eagle! Look at all the shiny rocks; I bet these are all magic stones."

"For sure they are," said Eagle. "At least that's what Seahawk said."

"What do you mean?"

"Seahawk said that everything here was magical and that you needed to come here to find the box and open six doors. Look, Chin, right here," pointed Eagle with his nose. "Right there is a box."

"That's exactly like the box I imagined," Chin whispered.

In front of the fountain's middle column rested a small box with a delicate butterfly engraved on the lid. The fountain had three columns, and the middle one was the tallest with sparkling water pouring down from it. It was strange that the box's lid was completely dry, even when it was partially submerged and water was splashing around it.

Chin stepped into the fountain, careful not to disturb the harmony of the rocks around it. He grabbed the box while holding the magic stone steady with his other hand.

He opened the lid, and a soothing light came from inside the box. The light's color matched the stone, and Chin saw that the wood inside the box was carved in an arrowhead shape that was a perfect match for his magic stone. He carefully placed the stone in position and closed the lid.

As soon as he picked up the box, he perceived something moving away from behind the tall columns.

He quickly moved his head to the right, focusing his eyes in the darkness behind the soft glow of the columns. He could see nothing but a huge shadow flying away, followed by hundreds of small shadows. They were too far away for him to decipher what they were.

A cold breeze and a subtle sound followed the shadows. It sounded like the wind moving through the branches of the old cedars in Chin's backyard. The shadows whispered things that he could not understand—a confusion of words and sounds.

"Frrr, flrrr, frrr, flrrr," was the sound, repeated again and again by the smaller shadows. The big shadow laughed while leading them to an obscure corner at the left side of the big cavern.

Everything was back to silence. Only the sound of the water splashing from the fountain filled the chamber, and Chin thought the shadows were gone.

But just as he thought this, suddenly the group of shadows returned, spinning in circles above his head like an airplane in a landing pattern. After several circles, the strange silhouettes soared off to the door at the center column and across the chest of the spearman guarding it, leaving a dark mark on the shiny armor of the guard. It looked like two letters: *S* and *L*.

Somehow Chin was not afraid. He was surprised because the shadows were similar to the ones he saw in his dreams. Somehow his dream had become real, he thought, or maybe he was still dreaming.

He was trying to figure it out when the joyful and familiar voice of Eagle interrupted his thoughts.

"Very beautiful box," said Eagle. "And it matches the stone; I guess Seahawk knew what he was talking about."

"Did you see that, Eagle?" Chin asked in amazement.

"What, the box? Why of course, Chin—what else?" asked Eagle.

"No, Eagle, I mean did you see the shadows?" asked Chin urgently.

"I'm afraid I did not," said Eagle. "I was too occupied drinking water from the fountain and finding a place where I could pee. You know a good dog has always to leave a mark on the special places we visit. As a matter of fact, now that you have learnt how to bark, you should learn how to mark your territory with pee. I can teach you that—"

"Eagle! I'm not joking; can you ever take anything seriously?"

"What for? Life is to have fun," said Eagle. "We must be outrageously happy!"

"Yes, I know ... sure," said Chin, with resignation.

"Well, Chin," continued Eagle, "do you think that's the box Seahawk was talking about? He was right ..."

"And I did a good job at visualizing things," interrupted Chin, forgetting for a moment about the shadows. "Hey, I deserve some recognition too."

Abruptly Chin covered his mouth with his hands, dropping the box on his lap.

"Eagle, we're talking human and dog talk, but I don't have the stone in my hand to give me those powers!"

26

"Yes," said Eagle cheerfully. "You are barking with a very good accent."

"Eagle, I don't bark," Chin insisted. "You know that—it's the stone!"

"Well, you don't have the stone anymore, and I can't speak human, so it must be that you're barking," replied Eagle, merrily chasing his reflection in the water.

"Maybe Seahawk or Super Abuelo can clarify things for us," said Chin. "Let's get out of here. I'm hungry, and Mom is waiting for us at the coffee shop, for sure. We can come back tomorrow."

"And now we know how to get here, and the place is marked with my pee—that will keep others away," added Eagle.

"Sure, Eagle," Chin said with a laugh. He was excited with the outcome of the morning. He had what he needed: the box for his magic stone.

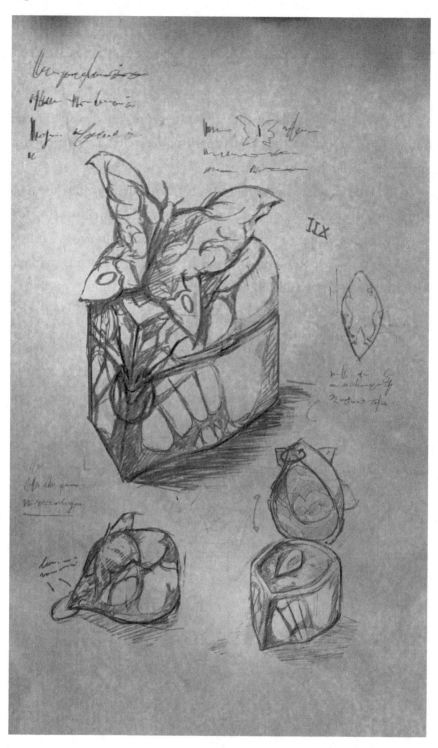

CHAPTER 5 ━━━━━

Back to Crack the Code

CHIN AND EAGLE WENT BACK. THEY saw letters carved into the stairs and painted in different colors. One by one, Chin counted the steps as he climbed up. When he wanted to calm down, he often concentrated his mind on doing mental math games. Counting things and finding hidden patterns or series was a favorite pastime for Chin.

"One, two, three—black P. Four, five, six, seven—red C. Eight, night, ten—black S. Eleven, twelve, thirteen, fourteen—red F. Twenty-eight—red C. Hmm, Eagle, can you see this pattern?" asked Chin.

"Actually I don't even know what a pattern is. Is it something we can eat? Because I'm hungry," replied Eagle.

"No, Eagle, it's not food—it's a pattern. It's a special array of numbers or objects following some sort of rule. I'll take note of this and talk later about it with my friend Xam. I bet he'll be able to help me solve this puzzle."

After twenty-eight steps, they were back in front of the magic door. The place for the missing knob was still glowing in the dark, and Chin knew what to do. After taking the stone out of the box, he pressed it firmly against the door and turned it counterclockwise.

Light filled the hallway, the door opened, and they were back at Carillon Point, just in time to hear the final notes of the ninth ring from the bells. It was somehow still nine o'clock!

The fishermen were still fighting the seagulls away, the boats were still cruising, the sun was still in the same spot in the sky, and Chin was still standing with his hand holding the stone, pointing north, at the very end of the shadow cast by the third column of the old carillon.

"Eagle, this is so weird. Look at the clock on top of the carillon; it's still nine o'clock! We haven't moved. But look—I have my box with me. It was real—it *is* real!"

"Yes, it was very real indeed. The stairs were real, the hall, the delicious water, and the magic door, everything *was* real, and Seahawk and Super Abuelo were right," Eagle replied calmly.

"Everything is still confusing to me, Eagle. Let's call Mom to take us home so we can rest and have a snack and then talk about this with Seahawk. I also want to talk to my friend Xam about the pattern we found."

Chin's mom stopped by the coffee shop one hour later and picked up Chin and Eagle. It was a short drive home, but the smooth buzz of the electric motor was like a sleeping potion for Eagle, and in a few minutes he was sound asleep on Chin's lap.

"It looks like you had a lot of fun," Mom said from the driver's seat. "Eagle is completely tuckered out!"

"Yeah, Mom, it was great," Chin replied. "A real adventure."

"What happened when you put the stone in the magical place?" Mom asked.

"Oh, Mom, I'm not sure you'd believe it. It was amazing—it was a secret entrance to a magical dimension, and I found this beautiful box!"

"Let me see it." Chin held up the box. "Well, it's certainly an interesting box, Chin, very old and rusty. Did you find that at the marina?"

"Rusty? Mom, can't you see the colors and the butterfly?"

"Now that you tell me, I suppose I can imagine it in my mind as a beautiful box with a colorful butterfly on the lid. But only in my imagination; my eyes can only see a rusty box, I'm afraid."

"Maybe you're right, Mom. Maybe what I'm seeing is beautiful in my imagination only."

Chin realized that his mom could not see the beautiful colors, just like she was not able to see the blue glow from the magic stone. He realized he had so many questions to ask Seahawk.

And he also needed to share the interesting pattern with his good friend Xam. He was sure the pattern had a meaning; it was not yet clear in his mind what the meaning was, but once he put that on paper and with the help of his friend, he felt sure he would solve the mystery. Maybe Seahawk knew something about the pattern and about the shadows too.

"Mom, do you have a pencil? I lost mine," Chin asked.

"Did you check inside your journal? You always put your pen in the small front pocket," his mother suggested.

"You're right, Mom ... here it is."

Chin wrote down the pattern in his journal. He also drew a sketch of the six columns and the words written at the doors. He was eager to meet with his friend Xam, who was a terrific brainstormer.

Chin pictured Xam stopping by his house that afternoon, as he hoped. It was easy for him to imagine things happening, just like the compass, the box, and his dad taking him to the marina. Somehow it seemed that when he wanted something, he was either able to get it or he got the means to get it or sometimes he got the right idea on how to get it. It had started in Arizona when he created that perfect square in a cloud and then the bow and arrow.

After that first experience in Arizona, he noticed that he was often able to win in board games when he really wanted to. He seemed to receive phone calls or emails from the people he was thinking about, and he always seemed to find the special tool, crayon, or book he was looking for by thinking about it. Sometimes it was like magic; sometimes it was a series of coincidences that led to the desired result.

He never paid much attention to it, as it was something natural for him; but lately, as he became older, he realized that not everybody was able to visualize things, so he decided not to talk much about it.

He reviewed his drawing and was pleased with it. He had captured the words, the number of steps, the number of doors, and took note of the colors. He closed his black journal and pet Eagle on his back.

"You can keep doing that," said Eagle. "I love it when you pet my back."

Chin smiled and thought how lucky he was to have found the magic stone and the magic box. He had a feeling it was only the beginning of more adventures to come.

As Mom drove down the street near their house, Chin smiled as he spotted his friend waiting for him at the front door. Xam was waving at them, and Chin could not wait to talk to him.

Chin opened the door of the car and Eagle jumped out, running in playful circles around Xam.

"Hi, Xam, I'm so happy you're here," Chin called out. "I found a cool pattern at the marina. Maybe we can decipher it together."

Chin didn't want to share the full details about his magic experience yet. *Maybe later*, he thought to himself.

"I knew it!" replied Xam. "I was just at home reading a good book when I felt like I just had to come over here. I was bummed when you weren't home, but then I saw your mom's car coming. So, let's see your pattern."

"Let's go in the house. I'm starving, and we can have a snack while we solve this puzzle," replied Chin.

Chin carefully put the magic box on the kitchen table and grabbed two dark chocolate bars. Xam looked at the box questioningly.

"What's that?" Xam asked Chin curiously. "Where did you find that old rusty box?"

"I found it at the marina. I think it's part of the puzzle," replied Chin, a bit disappointed that his friend couldn't see the colors and the soft glow of the box. "But first let me show you the pattern. It's here in my journal."

Chin opened the old black journal and quickly flipped the pages, finding the one where he took his notes. Xam and Chin each grabbed a piece of paper and started to make notes, writing down numbers, drawing lines connecting the numbers and words, and discussing their ideas.

The two boys had three golden rules for solving patterns: any idea was considered, no idea was ever a crazy idea, and there was no single answer to one problem. They knew they could always find more than one way to solve a puzzle.

"Look at this, Xam—the letters on the steps match the first letter of each one of the words written on the doors."

"Hey, that's true," said Xam. "But since the doors are arranged in a circle, there's no beginning or end—any door can be the first one. I think the steps give us some sort of order. There are twenty-eight steps, and there's a letter every third step and every fourth step, and that pattern repeats until the last step. Let's put that in order."

When they put that in order, the sequence started to make sense: three-black-P, seven-red-C, etc.

"Well, the first letter in the series is *P*," said Chin, "and since there is only one door's name that starts with *P*, looks like 'Propositum' is the first door."

"Yes, we solved it!" replied Xam.

But Chin wanted to know the meaning of the color pattern and the numbers. Maybe old Seahawk could help later.

CHAPTER 6 ━━━━━━

A Guardian Has Been Appointed

THAT AFTERNOON, CHIN TOOK HIS MAGIC box and went to the backyard to play with Eagle. Eagle was drinking water from the pond when old Seahawk landed by his side.

"Did you find the entrance using the magic stone as the key?" asked Seahawk.

"Yes we did," replied Eagle cheerfully. "But now Chin has more questions. I guess humans always want to ask questions."

"What questions do you have, young men?" Seahawk asked Chin and Eagle. "Do you want to know about the doors or about the other stones? Or about the magical fountain? Or maybe you got scared and you want to know about the Shadow Lord?"

"Shadow Lord?" asked Chin. "I certainly saw the shadow, and I saw the letters S and L marked on the shiny armor of the guard after the shadows went though him, but I thought it was just my imagination. It sounds dangerous. Actually I want to know about everything!"

"Of course you want to know everything, young man," Seahawk replied, chuckling. "And you deserve to know about it since you accepted becoming the key holder and the guardian of the stone."

Chin stared at old Seahawk, his eyes wide open. He was puzzled by his words. He wanted to know all the answers, but every time he found an answer, it opened the door for even more questions.

"Let me start by saying that it is a grand honor to be appointed a key holder and guardian of the stone," said Seahawk in a serious tone, almost whispering. "But it is just the beginning. To have the stone is just the first step. It gives you access to many places and allows you to talk to any living creature in this dimension and in many others. But it is a temporary gift. You must go through six challenges, solving six mysteries. In the process of doing that, you will get more temporary gifts, more powers, more keys, more magic stones and magical artifacts until you get to the final destination."

"What is the final destination? I am sure I can do it," Chin replied, excited by the possibility of more gifts and more adventures.

"Later you will learn what the final destination is, young man. I just want to warn you about the obstacles and perils you could face. It will not be an easy task. You are not the only key holder—there are 111 all over the world and there are magic doors in forty-nine cities. Few guardians manage to get past the first challenge, and no one has ever gone to the final one. The Shadow Lord keeps fighting back."

"And how can I win?" asked Chin.

"That you must answer by yourself. But we will help you. We have been watching you for a while, and we think you are ready. We knew you were ready long ago. Learning to visualize things was a first step in your training, and getting that bow and arrow was another step."

"And a very useful tool to battle the Shadow Lord and his legion of minions I might add," said Eagle cheerily. "I will show you how to use it. As a matter of fact, I would love to chew that bow right now."

"What do you mean by training?" Chin asked in confusion, ignoring Eagle's lightheartedness. "And what do you mean by *we*? And no, Eagle, I do not want you to chew my bow."

"Everything will be revealed at the proper time, Chin, but first you have to agree to be appointed guardian and key holder. Once you accept it, you cannot go back, unless you fail—"

"I am super ready!" Chin interrupted with excitement.

"I am glad you are. Because you actually accepted the moment you picked up the box from the magic fountain and put the magic stone inside. Open the box now."

When Chin opened the box, the stone was still there, with its now-familiar blue glow, but encrypted in the surface of the stone he found two unfamiliar words.

"*Ab Intra*. What does that mean?" asked Chin.

"It probably means that it's suppertime," joked Eagle. "I'm starving! I suppose the stone is smart enough to sense how hungry I am."

"Good try, Eagle, but I don't think so," replied Chin.

"Its meaning is the solution to the first challenge and the door to enter the six worlds," explained Seahawk. "You will learn more at a later stage; now I think you deserve some rest. You have to go back to the marina tomorrow at the same time you went today and go through the first challenge. Remember to bring your bow and arrow—not the toy, the real one you got from Forrest. He is one of us; he gave you the proper bow for the task."

"I'll be there," Chin promised. "Anything else I must know?"

"Be watchful of the type of challenge you will get into. Do you remember the colors on the pattern?"

"Yes I do; I have it here in my journal," said Chin, opening his black journal and showing old Seahawk the puzzle solved.

"Good work. Now remember this: black means that you will have help once you are inside. In those rooms we have managed to place a trained aid. But beware of the red ones. On those ones you will be on your own."

After saying this, Seahawk flew away, and Chin closed the box. He went to his room to pack his bow and arrow and everything else he needed: his compass, his flashlight, and his black journal. Once he was done packing, he felt cold. He thought it was because the window was open and it was already past seven p.m.

But when he stood up to close the window, he found it already closed. He turned back just in time to see a small shadow, just like the ones in the cavern, leaving his room through the back wall. It was repeating the same chant: frrr, flrrr, frrr, flrrr …

CHAPTER 7 ━━━━

Back in the Secret Cavern

IT WAS A RAINY DAY IN Kirkland. Chin and Eagle, wet to the bone, stood in front of the carillon at the marina. It was ten minutes to nine o'clock, and Chin was wondering how to discover the proper place to put the stone and open the magic door. The day was cloudy and dark, which made it hard to see the shadow cast by the third column.

"This is going to be hard, Eagle. How do we figure this out?"

"Next time I will pee in the right place so we can find it even when it's dark," Eagle said, chuckling.

"Is that the only solution you can think about? You dogs are obsessed with peeing and with eating," Chin replied.

"Is there anything else worth doing in life, my dear guardian? That is the joy of life—that and being outrageously happy over everything," Eagle concluded, jumping up to catch some raindrops in his open mouth.

Thinking about possible solutions, Chin saw Super Abuelo at the pier, chasing away other birds and trying to take the fresh bait from the fishermen's buckets.

"Eagle, let's go talk to Super Abuelo—maybe he knows how to open the door when there is no good sunlight," Chin said.

Chin ran across the pier; with only ten minutes left, he did not want to miss the opportunity to enter the secret cavern.

"Good morning, boys," said Super Abuelo. "I'm glad to see you back here; we're all very proud to have such a brave key holder and guardian of the stone."

"How do you know about it?" asked Chin.

"We all know, young man; we are a growing number or warriors. The Shadow Lord and his shadow minions will not keep doing harm for much longer, if you and other guardians succeed, of course. But hurry up; it is almost nine o'clock, and you need to get there and put the stone in the proper place to open the door."

"That's exactly the problem," replied Chin. "I can't find the place to put the stone because it's very cloudy and there isn't a good shadow."

"And he forgot to pee to mark the spot," added Eagle. "No wonder humans are always lost! Next time I'll take good care of marking the territory."

"Ab Intra," replied Super Abuelo.

"What do you mean, Super Abuelo? I know the stone has that weird scripture, but what I need to know is how to get back to the cavern."

"Ab Intra, young man. I cannot say more." And he flew away, chasing a couple of young seagulls.

"This is so disappointing. Eagle, c'mon boy, let's walk back to the carillon. We'll figure out something."

It was nine o'clock. The carillon started its song, announcing the time with each bell: one, two …

"What am I supposed to do? There is no clear shadow!" Chin called out desperately.

Three, four …

"Ab Intra … ab intra, what can that possibly mean?" asked Chin, opening the magic box and looking at the glowing magical stone.

Five, six …

It rained harder and harder, and the cold breeze from Lake Washington made Chin shiver. Eagle jumped around him, dancing under the rain. With the noise of the raindrops hitting the pavement, the drops pounding over his head, the noise of Eagle jumping and barking, the seagulls' cawing in the distance, the wind blowing stronger and stronger … it was harder and harder to concentrate.

Seven, eight …

"I'm almost out of time. Think, Chin, think, think," Chin said to himself, louder and louder, trying to overcome the noisy environment. "Think, Chin, think. I got it! A beautiful sunray coming from a small opening in the clouds … that's what I need, just a little ray. I just have to vaporize a bit of that cloud, just for few seconds. I need no more, not a fancy square, not a big magic trick, just a tiny piece of clean sky. I could use that strong wind to move things around a bit," concluded Chin looking hopefully at the cloudy sky.

Nine …

And there it was: a small but clean opening in the clouds, a beautiful ray of sun reaching the third column and a perfectly drawn shadow cast on the concrete floor.

Chin grabbed the stone from the box, took a look at the compass to find north and put the stone in the proper place, turning it counterclockwise.

The wind was gone, the rain over, the marina in silence, and Chin and Eagle were once more at the other side of the door, at the top of the stairs leading to the circular hall inside the cavern.

"Good work, Chin! How did you do that? By using Ab Intra?"

"I don't know, I still need to figure that out, but I think the stormy wind helped us by clearing the clouds at the very last moment."

"Or maybe you cleared the clouds using the wind, master?" asked a deep and unfamiliar voice. Eagle darted behind Chin's legs.

Chin looked around and saw that the giant statue of the guardian in front of the second door was talking to him. It was still made out of stone, but it was slowly moving its lips, and its eyes were looking at Chin.

With every word, dust and small rocks fell from its face. Chin could hear the noise of the stone cracking as the words were formed. Every movement created a cloud of dust and a cracking sound.

"What do you mean by clearing the clouds? And why do you call me master?" asked Chin, holding tight to the magic box, which was glowing even more intensely.

"Aren't you the master? Only a master can carry that box and that stone. Only a master can move stormy clouds like you did. And the masters always have a fierce guardian with them," the guardian said, looking at Eagle who was now at ease and sniffing at the feet of the enormous statue.

"This is certainly a smart guardian," said Eagle. "You can recognize a brave, trained, and loyal British soldier like me when you see one."

"Yes, right!" exclaimed Chin, smiling as he remembered that just thirty seconds ago, Eagle had been terrified at the voice of the statue and was hiding behind Chin's legs.

"And what am I supposed to do?" asked Chin.

"Master, I will open the door for you—your first challenge waits behind this door. And your reward will be waiting for you here, if you ever come back."

"What do you mean, if I ever come back?"

"I am not authorized to say more; are you ready, master?"

Chin hesitated. He was eager to learn what adventure waited for them at the other side of the door, but he wanted for sure to be able to come back.

"We are!" said Eagle and Chin at the same time.

The giant statue lurched forward, with dust and rocks crumbling around as it pushed open the door with the word *Propositum* encrypted with silver letters in the center.

"What does 'propositum' mean?" asked Chin.

"You will learn that inside, master; I cannot say more. Just use the magic blue stone as your guide once you are inside. It will guide you to the hermit where the secret to the challenge lies. Good luck, master. This door will be sealed until you complete the challenge or until you fail and abandon the room through the smoky tunnel; there is no other way out."

"What if I get into trouble? Seahawk told me about a secret aid for some challenges, and this is a black challenge."

"I almost forgot that—yes, you might find a secret aid inside … if it has not been defeated already. That happens sometimes."

The guardian held the door open. As soon as Chin and Eagle crossed to the other side, the heavy door closed behind them and after a few seconds dissolved in the air. There was no way back.

CHAPTER 8 ⎯⎯⎯

Shadows Everywhere

CHIN OPENED THE BOX AND THE light of the magic stone pointed northeast. He looked around him. It was a familiar place; he was back in Kirkland at the old marina, the street still wet from the storm, but it was not raining anymore.

Chin was confused; he expected a magical place, maybe a cavern or a castle or some dungeons or a whole underground city beneath the roots of the trees and the city water lines. Anything but going back to Kirkland!

"Well, this is quite disappointing, Chin, don't you think?" asked Eagle.

"I'm not sure; it looks like Kirkland, but there's something strange—something I can't explain."

Chin listened to the familiar sounds: the seagulls squalling, the fishermen talking, and the buzz of the boats on the lake. He closed the lid of the box and went to the pier to sit down and think.

As he walked, he saw a kid from his school fishing at the pier. Chin approached him.

The kid whispered something, talking to himself. When Chin was ready to say hi, he saw a shadow to the left of the boy. Chin stopped and looked around.

"Eagle! Can you see that?" whispered Chin.

"Yes, there are shadow minions everywhere, or almost everywhere."

"Yes, look around; there's one shadow to the left of many of these kids. And look at the carillon—there is only one column and one bell!"

Everything was exactly the same: he was sure he was at Carillon Point, the old marina in Kirkland, but instead of the six columns and six bells, there was only one. Chin also noticed that everybody was talking aloud; or at least he heard everybody talking.

He was now close enough to make out what his school friend was saying. "Today's a very bad day; I don't know why I came here to fish. Of course I'm not gonna catch anything; I'm no good at this—I don't know what I was thinking!"

"Hi, Ekim! You're not a bad fisherman," said Chin. "Just be patient."

"Good to see you here, Chin. But what do you mean? I know I'm not a bad fisherman!"

When Chin heard Ekim talking, he realized that his friend had not been talking to him before; Ekim had been thinking, and Chin had been able to hear his thoughts. Chin suddenly realized that he could hear the thoughts of every kid at the marina!

"Yes, I know," said Chin, nervously. "Well, see you later. I have to take Eagle back home. Good luck, and try to catch a big one!"

Chin ran toward the lonely column at the center of the marina and again opened the lid of his box. The magic stone pointed again to the northeast.

"Let's go, Eagle," Chin said urgently. "We have to find the hermit and learn what we're supposed to do here. This is very strange … maybe we'll find some answers there."

Chin and Eagle walked for more than two miles. On their path they crossed a park near the little school that Chin attended. Chin and Eagle heard the thoughts and the conversations of all the kids playing a soccer game at the big field. Some kids had shadow minions by their sides; the shadow minions were always whispering something. Chin saw a dark cloud surrounding the kids the minions were talking to.

One of the kids playing soccer kept hiding behind other kids, avoiding his teammates, as if afraid of getting the ball and making a mistake. All the other kids were happy and smiling, playing with joy and confidence.

This kid was smiling too, but a shadow minion was always by his side, and when the ball was close to the kid, the minion whispered things, seeming to make the kid move away to avoid contact. Chin was a soccer fan, and he was puzzled by that strange behavior. He got closer to the big field.

"I'm not good at this!" the boy said miserably. "If I get the ball I'll kick it badly and my friends will laugh at me. I really want this game to be over."

"Flrrr, frrr, flrrr, frrr," whispered the shadow minion to the boy.

"I can't do it better … I wish I could, but I just know I'll kick the ball out of the big field or, even worse, I'll give it to an opponent and my team will lose because of me!" the boy said grimly.

"Flrrr, frrr, flrrr, frrr." The minion continued with its chant.

"Eagle, can you hear that?" Chin asked. "The kid is having lots of negative thoughts, and his thoughts get more and more negative every time the minion whispers. I could hit that stupid minion with my rock!"

"I can bark and scare him," Eagle suggested. "I bet you that minions are afraid of brave guardian dogs like me. After all, I was trained by Scotland Yard, the finest police department in Europe."

"Yeah right," said Chin. "I'm sure you could take care of that, but let's keep walking and find the hermit; we have a purpose."

They walked for another mile, past the big field, past the woods, through the forest of blackberries, scotch brooms, and stinging nettles, and under the protective shade of big cedars, maples, madronas, and douglas fir trees.

The vegetation got very dense, and they walked slowly to avoid the thorn bushes. There was no path to follow, and their only guide was the blue light of the magic stone that pointed northeast like a strong laser beam coming out of a light saber.

CHAPTER 9 ────────

The Challenge Revealed

AFTER A LONG WALK, THEY FOUND what they thought was a cave, but as they got closer, they realized it was a hole carved inside a big tree. It was probably caused by a fire after lightning struck it. The tree was at least twelve feet in diameter, and the entrance to the natural grotto was about five feet wide.

From the outside, they saw a familiar soft, blue light emanating from within the grotto, but the interior still looked very dark.

Once they went inside, and as soon as the light from the magic stone hit the back wall of the grotto, everything lit up, revealing a small circular hall surrounded by the black walls of burned-out wood turned into charcoal.

At the center of the circle, Chin saw a chest carved in brown stone. Its silver lid opened up when Chin and Eagle got closer to it.

"Wow, this is very cool—I bet there's something for us in that chest. This must be what the guardian asked us to look for. Do you agree, Eagle?"

"Most definitively. And there's lot of good bark to chew on while we explore the contents of the chest. Do you want some? It's very tasty. The ashes give the bark a delicious smoky flavor that reminds me of my puppyhood in England."

"No thanks, Eagle, I'll pass on that. You chew on it while I rest here a minute. I'm very tired."

Chin found a comfortable bench to sit on. He put his bow, his quiver with seven arrows, and his backpack on top of the bench. Sitting by the old tree gave him time to relax and think about all the magic things that had happened so far.

He was still disturbed by the shadow minions affecting the confidence of the kid playing soccer at the big field. He also realized that it was a shadow minion who was responsible for the lack of confidence in his friend Ekim fishing at Lake Washington.

Chin was not fearful, but the shadow minions disturbed him everywhere: in his dreams, at his house, when he first picked up his box at the magic hall—there was always a shadow minion around.

After resting for a few minutes, Eagle interrupted Chin's thoughts.

"I'm ready," said Eagle. "The bark was delicious, and I found plenty of fresh water in a creek behind the tree. I also went out and peed all around; this is our territory now. No creature would dare to come nearby because they'll smell the presence of a fearless Cavalier King Charles Spaniel."

"Um, okay, whatever you say, Eagle. Let's take a look at the chest and see what's inside it."

Inside the chest, Chin saw two tablets made out of stone: one with a riddle and the other one with just an arrowhead-shaped mark on the surface, like the mark where he put his magic stone to enter the magic cave.

From a red mother and a white father
Crafted by the old chief
White thunders will fly
From the guardian to the dark
The doubtful shadows will fade
For joy and happiness to reign
Ab Intra

Chin read that message again and again. He was sure it was the secret challenge, but he could not decipher its meaning.

"Eagle, I have no idea what this means; and there's that weird phrase again: Ab Intra. What are we supposed to do with this?"

"I'm sure you can figure it out, Chin, although it's too bad that your old friend Forrest isn't here; you said the chief was good with riddles."

"Yep, he was. He told me many stories and riddles when I met him in Arizona last fall. He told me beautiful stories about his tribe, about his trip to the Red Rock Canyons to grab special wood for making my bow ... for ... Eagle, you are a genius!"

"Am I? Of course I am ... Hmm, can you tell me why?"

"You are a genius, Eagle," repeated Chin again and again. "Forrest is the answer! He's the chief who crafted my bow made out of white wood that comes from a cave in the Red Rock Mountains. I have to use the bow and arrow to vaporize the bad shadows: the shadow minions. That's our challenge!"

"Oh, I see. Well yes, I am a genius indeed. But what does Ab Intra have to do with it?"

"I don't know, Eagle; we'll figure it out later. Let's run back to the big field or the marina and find the shadows! I have no time to lose right now; let's run back!"

"Okay, master, whatever you say. One more question: What about the other tablet?"

"It doesn't matter, Eagle. Let's put both tablets in my backpack and we can check that later. I want to battle the Shadow Lord and his minions now. I've been waiting for a while to have a good fight using my special bow and silver arrows. This is going to be awesome!"

CHAPTER 10

A Small Win and a Setback

CHIN AND EAGLE WENT BACK, FOLLOWING the path signaled by the magic stone. As they got closer to the end of the woods, Chin felt his heart rate increasing, and he clenched his teeth in determination. Even when racing past the thorn bushes, he didn't feel the thorns hurting him or tearing at the sleeves of his jacket.

He didn't even pay attention to the small red drops surfacing on the skin of the back of his hands. His anticipation of the battle made him unconscious of those minor injuries. He was ready, and so was Eagle running by his side.

In the distance, they heard the voices of the kids playing in the big field. The soccer game was coming to an end, and they could tell from the scoreboard that it was tied at three points for each team.

The crowd was cheering every movement from the players, every kick, every pass. Chin was focused on his mission, and in his mind, he mixed fantasy with reality; he imagined the crowd cheering him on, cheering for him to fight the shadow minions.

The shadow minion was still bothering that poor kid, destroying his confidence. The kid was sweating; his face was not joyful anymore. The shadows surrounding his body were now completely black, and he was having more and more negative thoughts, terrified that his team could lose the game because of him, mortified by what the crowd would say or think about him.

"I can't do this, oh please, please don't pass the ball to me. We'll lose if you do. I'm bad at playing soccer! Please don't see me—I am invisible, I am not here, don't pass me the stupid ball ..."

The kid kept repeating those negative thoughts, barely walking, moving around in awkward ways, trying to look like a bad choice for passing the ball to.

Chin got close enough to see the shadow minion as a perfect target; he decided to hide behind a big old madrona tree and gently put his backpack on the ground. He took his arrow and put the magic stone inside the central cavity of the bow.

It was a perfect fit as he learned before, but this time, when he inserted it, the whole bow glowed in the familiar and soothing blue light. Chin felt the bow vibrating in his hand; the stone gave the bow a new energy, a new feeling, and a very cool look.

The shadow minion looked at Chin and smiled, as if challenging Chin to do something. It was an arrogant smile, and while the minion had a smoky and dark face, Chin could see two red eyes floating in what must have been its equivalent of a face. He heard the familiar chant coming from the minion, though its usual noise morphed into words:

"Frrr, flrrr, frrr, flrrr ... You are no match for me, little boy. Go home and play with your little toy dog. I am busy here with this kid, and once I am finished with him, I will take care of you, so run away while you can ..."

Chin did not move and instead merely stared at the minion. Eagle did the same, with a fierce determination that Chin had never seen before in his loyal friend.

"I am not scared of you, little minion," Chin said firmly. "I have been appointed as the guardian, and I have a mission to accomplish, so you'd better run before I use my magic arrow."

Chin spoke while grabbing one silver arrow from his quiver. His right arm described an elegant circle, and the arrow was in position, ready to be fired. When Chin tensed the cord, the silver arrow burst into blue flames, making Chin yelp and almost drop it.

"Frrr, flrrr, frrr, flrrr," said the minion, his red eyes transfixed on Chin's face.

"Eagle, what do I do now?" Chin whispered frantically. "What if I hit the kid instead of the minion? And now this thing is in flames! Is this safe at all? What am I doing here? I must be crazy!"

Chin was now under the spell of the shadow minion and started to doubt his own abilities.

Suddenly, a huge bald eagle soared across the sky, above the top of the big madrona tree. It was Chin's favorite animal, and it was repeating again and again the same words with a powerful rhythm:

"Ab Intra, Ab Intra, Ab Intra ..."

It was the secret aid! Listening to those words succeeded in distracting Chin from the dark chant coming from the shadow minion. Chin focused again on his task. He pulled back his right hand three more inches, stretching the cord of the bow to its maximum.

His left arm was trembling with energy, and the arrow was now pure flames; it barely even looked like an arrow at all. The shadow minion increased the volume of his chant:

"Frrr, flrrr, frrr, flrrr," said the minion, with the red and smoky eyes focused on Chin.

"Ab Intra, Ab Intra, Ab Intra," sang the bald eagle, Chin, and Eagle in chorus.

"Frrr, flrrr, frrr, flrrr," repeated the shadow minion, now moving fast toward Chin, getting bigger and bigger as it got closer and closer.

"Ab Intra, Ab Intra, Ab Intra ..."

The shadow minion was very close, about thirty feet from Chin. Chin could not hold the arrow anymore; his arms were extremely tired from holding the stretched bow. But Chin waited a little bit more ... twenty feet ...

I can do it, thought Chin. *Forrest made this special arrow just for me, I have the magic stone, and I am a guardian. I can do this ... Come closer, just a bit closer, little friend. I am going to beat you!*

"Frrr, flrrr, frrr, flrrr—you are no match for me!"

Fifteen feet, it was now close enough. Chin opened his right hand, releasing the arrow, which flew quickly, thanks to the power of the stretched cord. The flames got bigger and blue sparks marked the traveled path through the air. Chin held his breath. The arrow instantly connected with the chest of the shadow minion. It hit perfectly what was supposed to be the heart and then passed through, disappearing.

The bald eagle sang louder, and Eagle was singing too. But Chin was so focused that he could hear nothing.

He was captivated by how the shadow minion changed color, from a deep black to a pure and glowing light blue. The minion was floating in front of Chin—not moving, not chanting, but just hovering in the air.

Chin relaxed his body, relaxed his jaw, his arms, his hands. The bow dropped out of his right hand, and drops of sweat covered his face. He was completely focused on the immobile minion. Then the noise and cheering from the crowd brought him back to his senses.

"Go, Odlanor, go for it!" cheered the crowd.

"Yes, I can do it, I can do it. My friends taught me this play many times. I can do this!" Chin heard the boy say, and he was happy to see how the kid was gaining confidence, how the dark shadow surrounding him started to vanish, and how positive thoughts were finally coming from the boy's mind.

"I will pretend to kick the ball with my right foot, then stop, move to the left, and kick it hard with my left foot toward the left side of the goalie. I can do this; I can see the ball hitting the net and the crowd saying my name. Sorry, goalie, nothing personal, but I am a winner today," the boy concluded triumphantly.

And saying that, Odlanor hit a perfect shot that fooled the goalie of the opposing team and became the last and winning point just five seconds before the end of the game.

"I'm good, I am really good, I'm great, we are really great," said Odlanor loudly while dancing a wild victory dance with his friends.

Chin was happy to see the boy regaining his self-confidence. He remembered how he had doubted himself just a few minutes ago and how once he put his positive thoughts in his mind again, he overcame fear and won over the minion.

"Flrrr, frrr, flrrr, frrr …"

Chin turned back to the minion and saw that it was gradually turning back to grey while whispering its chant. After a few seconds, it was again very dark, though not as black as it was before. Its voice was also different, less powerful, but its eyes were still flaming red.

56

"Flrrr, frrr, flrrr, frrr. I told you—you are not a match for me, little boy. You simply got lucky. I just need to rest for a while in the house of the Shadow Lord. Goodbye for now—but be ready for me. I will be back."

And the minion disappeared into the forest through the thorn bushes and huge trees.

"Well, this is quite disappointing," said Eagle. "Maybe you need to recharge the stone at some electrical outlet?" He barked at the last sight of the minion in the forest.

"Don't be silly, Eagle. There must be an answer. We did something wrong."

"Indeed, master, you made a small mistake, but do not worry, this is just a small setback," said the bald eagle, who now rested on top of the madrona tree.

"What mistake? Who are you? What does Ab Intra mean?" asked Chin.

"One question at a time, master. I am your secret aid for this challenge. Would you think we would leave you alone?"

"Well, of course not. Seahawk did say something about a secret aid on the black challenges and not on the red ones, but—"

"But nothing, master. I will tell you more about me later, after you finish this task. Now we have to hurry and complete the mission while the minion is still weak."

"What am I supposed to do?"

"Find the chest with no lid and no key, master—the answer lies within," said the bald eagle beginning to take off in flight. "Use the magic stone to find the minion once you read the message inside the chest. I will be waiting for you there; I have to keep an eye on him."

"Wait—one last question. What does Ab Intra mean?"

"We'll discuss that later ..." and the bald eagle disappeared between two white clouds.

Chin sat down in the shade of the madrona tree. He was exhausted and hungry. From his backpack he retrieved some chocolate chip cookies for himself and some doggie treats for Eagle. He studied the second tablet. It was as long as his foot and as wide as his opened right hand.

The tablet was made out of a beautiful brown stone, probably fossilized material—something he'd learned about from the Rock Man when he attended geology camp at the Olympic Peninsula in Port Angeles. The Rock Man was a very well known geologist in the Pacific Northwest.

The tablet was almost two inches thick with a beautiful white line around the edge, as if it were separating the tablet into two thin faces. He looked at the arrowhead-shaped mark and realized that probably his magic stone was also a switch to turn the tablet on or to reveal a message.

"I think I got it, Eagle—it's just a matter of using the magic stone as the key! Just like we did to open the secret door to the underground world."

"But of course, Chin. I knew that; I just wanted you to find the answer by yourself. In my extensive training as a secret agent in London I was taught how to recognize secret keys—"

"Sure," interrupted Chin, not taking Eagle seriously. "But we have no time to learn about your special training. Let's see what secret we reveal."

Chin unstuck the stone from his bow. When he did, the bow went back to its normal wood color and regular appearance; the blue glow went away with a buzz that reminded Chin of the sound of a light saber being turned off in the *Star Wars* movies. He put the stone inside the carving on the tablet.

"A perfect fit, Eagle—it's a totally perfect fit!" Chin said in delight.

When the stone was locked on the tablet, a two-word encryption appeared on the surface of the tablet, beneath the stone: *Ab Intra*.

"C'mon, not again," Chin said in disappointment. "I already know that Ab Intra is a secret word, but how does that help me to fight the shadow minion?"

Chin dropped the tablet on his lap and stared at those words while eating his chocolate chip cookies. Eagle had finished eating his treats and drinking water from the nearby creek and was now sleeping by his side.

The kids were gone; after finishing the soccer game some went back to their houses, and some had switched to playing games on the big field and at the basketball court nearby. It was a peaceful afternoon, and Chin focused on deciphering this new message. After ten minutes of listening to Eagle's relaxed breathing, and tired from his long walk and the battle with the minion, he fell asleep too.

CHAPTER 11 ────────

The Final Clue Leads to the Big Battle

CHIN DREAMED OF THOUSANDS OF ROCKS, and in his dream a professor asked him about the different types of rocks—sedimentary, igneous, and metamorphic—and about places, sizes, shapes, and categories. It was a confusing dream, and Chin woke up disturbed by its images.

When he awoke, he could sense the answer to his problem was somehow hidden in that dream. Forrest, the old chief of the Hopi tribe, had told him once to meditate to find the answer to his problems, but he found meditation to be quite a challenge: it was too difficult to think about nothing and remain quiet.

Instead he found that after trying to meditate he often fell asleep and in his dreams he could find answers to his challenges and problems. Since he often forgot what the dreams were about, he decided to write things down in his black journal for future reference.

Chin grabbed his pen and wrote down all the details he could remember. He read it a couple times, and after a few minutes, he realized he had found the answer.

"Eagle, wake up, I think I have a clue, but I need help. What have you got?"

"I was in deep meditation trying to find an answer, but you interrupted me."

"Meditation? I think you were snoring pretty loudly, my friend," said Chin sarcastically.

"You underestimate my capacity to enter into a profound state of meditation. Tell me what you found."

"Well, I'm not sure, but in my dream I was discussing rocks with a professor, and he asked many questions ..."

"You mean a professor like the Rock Man?"

"Of course, Eagle, you're right again! It was the Rock Man in my dream ... maybe the answer is in something he taught me about rocks, but what it could be?"

"Well," Eagle began, "I can tell you the tablet is a brown rock."

Chin grabbed the tablet and looked at the white line that divided the tablet in two. He smiled triumphantly and took the magic stone out of the carved mark.

"You're right again," said Chin. "This is a beautiful brown tablet, and brown stone often means one thing: fossils. I don't know what Ab Intra means, but I'm almost positive that the secret is inside the tablet. This is the secret chest with no handles, lid, or key."

Chin remembered how the Rock Man always amazed kids by showing them what they thought were regular rocks and then giving the rocks a whack with his hammer, opening them to reveal beautiful fossils or crystals inside.

"But if that's true, then what does Ab Intra mean?" asked Eagle.

"I don't know, but I guess we'll learn later. Let me just try opening up this tablet. I just need to find a hammer. We can't get out of here until we complete our mission. I just need a small hammer—I'm sure we'll find one around here."

Chin put all his belongings in his backpack, took his bow and quiver, and walked away, not knowing where he was going, just knowing he needed a hammer.

After a short walk, he saw a familiar face. It was Nek, a retired architect who worked as volunteer fixing things for the neighborhood kids. Whether it was the swing set at the big field or the tree house at school or the old library nearby, Nek was always fixing something.

"Hi, Chin, what are you doing here? Are you enjoying your spring break?" Nek asked.

"Yes, very much. Right now I'm looking for some rocks, trying to find some fossils to share with my friends and my teacher, Mrs. Sallice, next week."

"Oh, great idea. I'm trying to fix the old slide. I just need to put in some reinforcement nails, and it'll be better than new."

"Nails? That means you have a hammer," said Chin with a big smile.

"Well, of course I do. In fact, I have more than one hammer in this big toolbox."

"Can I borrow one? I need one for cracking open the sedimentary rocks to find fossils inside, but I forgot my hammer."

"Sure you can. Take this one with you, and if I'm not around when you finish, just leave it by the front door of my house."

"Thank you very much, Nek," Chin exclaimed.

Chin took the hammer and returned to the forest, beyond the thorn bushes, where he and Eagle could be alone to open the tablet and reveal the secret.

Once in a safe place away from everybody, Chin took the tablet out of his backpack and tapped alongside the white border. Each tap produced a hollow, dry sound that confirmed to Chin the stone was indeed some sort of chest. But after several minutes of tapping on it, he still could not open the tablet.

"Maybe you should try with the stone in place," suggested Eagle.

"Why of course!" Chin responded with excitement. "That must be a security measure, to make sure that only somebody with the magic stone could open it. I should've thought about that."

Chin took the magic stone and carefully put it in the carved mark on the tablet. The tablet buzzed on, displaying the blue glow. The insertion of the stone had momentarily changed the tablet's composition and thereby allowed it to break apart. This time, with the first soft tap on the side, the tablet cracked along the white line, and a shiny blue light filtered through the cracks.

Chin opened it up carefully. It was so shiny that it took a while for his eyes to get used to the brilliant light and see the interior of the tablet. When his eyes adjusted, he could see that the tablet was full of tiny crystals arranged in a spiral pattern. At the center of the spiral was a bigger white crystal in the shape of an egg and as big as his thumb.

Chin carefully lifted the egg-shaped crystal and noticed words carved on its surface—tiny words that he was not able to read. He remembered his compass in his backpack. It had a whistle, a thermometer, and also a small magnifying glass. Chin used it to read the encryption.

"Look at this, Eagle," said Chin, holding the magnifying glass close to the carved surface of the crystal egg. "We're ready to go and find that shadow minion, and we have to hurry up."

Chin read aloud the encryption on the crystal egg:

Seven silver thunders it will take
Through the center of the shade.
Waste no time and have no delays.
Hear nothing but yourself,
Or your life will be at stake.
Ab Intra

CHAPTER 12 ━━━━━

A Battle of Body and Mind

AFTER A FEW MINUTES FOLLOWING THE path indicated by the magic stone, Chin and Eagle heard two distinct sounds: kids playing in the distance, and the chant of the shadow minion.

Chin stopped to plan his attack. He wasn't sure how the encounter with the shadow minion would go, but he was clear on his mission: six more silver thunders needed to go through the minion's heart. That meant six more silver arrows to complete the seven thunders suggested by the riddle written on the surface of the crystal egg.

He stopped and took the backpack off his back and grabbed an arrow with his left hand. With his right hand, he locked the magic stone into the bow, and it activated the soft blue glow of magical power. The energy and the soft vibration once again buzzed through his arm.

His heart pounded harder and faster in anticipation of the imminent battle. Eagle was ready too, with his eyes locked on the shadow that was floating around the kids in the distance.

"How do you shoot six arrows at once?" asked Eagle.

"I don't know," Chin answered. "Should I shoot all the arrows at once or one by one? One by one, I think. That's why the riddle asks for no delays. I need to be a fast archer and an accurate one too."

"Accurate for sure," Eagle pondered. "You have only six arrows left in your quiver."

Chin and Eagle walked slowly, tiptoeing on the soft grass and hiding behind bushes and trees. They wanted to get as close as possible to the shadow minion before starting the fight. Chin was tense in anticipation, and the bow vibrated more and more as they got closer to the kids.

They were close enough to hear the children's chat and the continuous chant of the shadow minion. The minion was turning back into its deep black shade, slowly recovering from the previous battle.

"We have to attack soon, Eagle," Chin whispered, looking at the shadow minion. "It's regaining all its strength. We have to be fast."

"Indeed you have to act quickly, master," whispered the bald eagle nearby. Chin hadn't even heard him land. "The seven arrows must go through its heart, or you'll fail and you'll meet a disturbing destiny back in the hallway and through the smoky tunnel."

"What destiny?" Chin asked worriedly.

"There's no time to discuss that," the bald eagle replied. "Focus on your task and believe in yourself, master. Ab Intra, Ab Intra, Ab Intra. I'll be watching you. Just remember to bring the tablets with you always. Those tablets are made out of sediments from the purple sea and are stronger than any element known by humans and even stronger than your magic arrows."

Chin walked a few more steps, focusing on the distant shadow while trying hard not to be seen by the shadow minion or the children. He didn't have time to explain to the children what he was doing there with a shiny blue bow and silver arrows.

Back in a corner of the big field, by the old library building, Chin saw his schoolmates Haras and Acire and a few other girls talking together. The shadow minion danced around Haras and through her.

"I think I shouldn't go on that field trip," Haras was saying. "My food allergies will make me sick, and I won't be able to have fun. I'm almost sure something really bad will happen."

"But Mrs. Sallice will take care of you, Haras," reassured Acire. "Please come with us—it's our last year together before going to different middle schools next year. And besides," she added, "if you don't go to camp, who's gonna tell us all ghost stories every night? You're the best storyteller in our class."

"I just can't do it; I'm too afraid. Something bad could happen, and the camp is too far away. Just thinking about it makes me sick—look at the rash on my right arm!"

Chin and Eagle got closer and closer. Chin hated to see how much the shadow minion was destroying the confidence of his friend. Chin took one silver arrow from his quiver and put it in position, ready to fire. He just needed to get closer—no more than fifteen feet away from the shadow minion to be sure he wouldn't miss the shot.

At twenty feet, he stepped on a broken branch, and the sound pierced the silence like thunder before a big storm.

"Shh, somebody's coming," whispered Acire.

Chin was quick enough to hide behind an old tool shed next to the old library building. But he wasn't fast enough to avoid the suspicious look of the shadow minion.

"I see you do not give up easily, young boy," snarled the shadow minion. "I will take care of you and your toy dog. And this time your eagle friend won't be of much help."

He pointed to an old pine tree. At the top of the tree, Chin saw a dark, semitransparent sphere floating in the air, trapping the bald eagle inside.

The bald eagle was gesticulating, opening and closing its mouth, and flapping its wings. But no sound could pass through the magic sphere that surrounded it. Their secret helper was captive, and Chin and Eagle were alone.

The shadow minion moved fast toward Chin, not giving him time to think or plan. When Chin felt he was ready to react it was already too late—the minion went through him, leaving a bad metallic taste in his mouth and clouding his vision for a few seconds.

Without thinking, Chin fired the silver arrow. It flew through the sky, bursting into glowing white flames and disappearing in the middle of the air, not even scratching the minion. Chin knew he was in trouble, and the bald eagle was not there to help.

"I guess I win this time, little boy," the shadow minion called out, cackling. "Frrr, flrrr. Frrr, flrrr …"

What do I do now? Chin thought to himself in a panic. "Only five arrows left!" he said aloud. "I guess I'm actually a failure; maybe I wasn't a good choice for this task after all. Maybe I'm really not a good guardian."

"Hey, stop that," said Eagle. "You're still the best—you can do it! Push that grey cloud away from your thoughts and fire off the other five arrows. Ab Intra!"

Chin took a deep breath, grabbed another arrow from his quiver, and fired a perfect shot. The flaming arrow went through the center of the shadow minion and exploded, as before, in midair, but this time making the minion appear whiter.

"Again, Chin—shoot again!" cried Eagle.

Chin continued in fast and coordinated movements. He was like an automated archery machine, shooting arrow after arrow, each one piercing the center of the shadow.

Now the shadow minion could hardly move, its eyes losing their powerful look, its formerly harsh words transformed to a barely audible whisper.

Arrows number four, five, and six all burst into flames. The school children in the distance could just see a fireworks show coming from behind the trees. They were puzzled but too afraid to go there and take a closer look.

"Look at the bald eagle!" called Eagle. "The bubble surrounding it is almost completely transparent, as transparent as the shadow minion. You can still win this battle, Chin—I'm sure you can cream that silly shadow minion!"

But Chin was hesitant to fire his seventh and final arrow. He had wasted his second shot, yet he was sure somehow he was going to be able to complete the task. But without the disturbing influence of the shadow minion, Chin suddenly felt newly relaxed and confident, focused on his goal.

"I need another arrow, I need another arrow," Chin said to himself softly.

The shadow minion started the recovery process; this time it was slower—he was weaker after five arrows had gone through him than he'd been after just one.

"I need another arrow ... I need another arrow," Chin repeated.

The bald eagle moved inside the spherical trap with its mouth wide open and clearly shouting something while looking at Chin and Eagle.

"I need another arrow—I need to complete the mission, I need to complete the mission," Chin repeated.

Eagle was quiet, still, with his eyes locked on the bald eagle, his head tilted toward it, trying to hear its voice.

"Stay quiet, master," said Eagle. "I think I can hear something..."

After a few seconds, Eagle jumped from Chin's side. He ran back to the old madrona tree where they had left the backpack and the tablets. He retrieved the old tablet with his mouth.

The bald eagle was now clearly exhausted inside the sphere, slumped against the wall, but with a hopeful and relaxed look on its face. Eagle ran fast and placed himself behind the shadow minion. Chin was perplexed by the dog's behavior and kept repeating the same words in his mind:

I need to complete the task. We will win. I need to complete the task. We will win ...

"Fire the last arrow, Chin," shouted Eagle. "Fire it now; trust me!"

Chin looked up at the shadow still floating before him. The shadow minion was between Eagle and Chin, defenseless but gradually recovering and smiling at the unfortunate situation of Chin not having enough arrows to complete his task.

Chin decided it was now or never: he'd trust Eagle. He drew back the bowstring and released. With a *thwang*, the flaming arrow sped through the air, hissed through the shadow, and shot toward

Eagle, who leapt five feet in the air and released the tablet from his mouth.

It was an amazing five-foot jump, certainly not a world record, but an amazing feat for a one-foot-tall Cavalier King Charles dog. At the peak of his jump, he opened his mouth, releasing the tablet.

Chin and the shadow minion watched what happened next as if it were in slow motion. When the shadow minion realized what was going to happen, it was already too late. The glowing arrow hit the tablet in midair and bounced back in an astounding perfect one-hundred-eighty-degree angle.

The smile disappeared from the minion's face as the last arrow was suddenly speeding back toward him. It blasted through him a second time, completing the seven shots—the seven silver thunders brightening his darkness.

It was a huge and colorful explosion. The light went through the trees, the bushes, the buildings, even through Eagle and Chin, who were blinded momentarily by the powerful beam. It felt as if a luminous tornado had gone through their bodies and their faces.

Chin noticed a burning sensation on the right side of his neck, below his ear. He thought it was probably some debris from the explosion scratching his skin a bit.

"Thank you," said the minion strangely and unexpectedly. His face was not smoky anymore, his eyes turned blue, like the magic stone, and what was not much more than a shadow, turned into something transparent, like water standing still in the middle of the air. "I am grateful to be liberated from the spell of the Shadow Lord. Now children can visualize without fear … Ab Intra …"

And the shadow minion disappeared, leaving behind a trail of tiny crystals that fell to the ground.

"Wow, we are certainly amazing warriors!" said Eagle. "I guess that training at Scotland Yard in London was useful after all. Did you see my masterful jump? It felt like three hundred feet!"

"Well, maybe not three hundred …" Chin said with a smile. "But it was an awesome jump, Eagle. Why did you do that?"

"Because he has a very fine ear," said the bald eagle, free now from the dark bubble. "He heard me even through the thick walls of that bubble. I was shouting: tablet, tablet, tablet …"

"Yes, and I recalled what you said about the tablet being stronger than anything made by humans or any of our magic weapons, so I figured out the arrow would bounce from it."

"Good thinking," said Chin.

"Now you can go back to the secret hall, master; your reward is waiting for you," said the bald eagle.

"What reward?" asked Chin. "And wait, you have to tell me a couple things before you go."

"I'm just a secret helper in this challenge, and my mission is accomplished. Now go and get your reward. The door has been unlocked, and you can get back using the stone as your key. I will probably see you on a future mission."

"More challenges? I need a break now," Chin protested.

"Oh, this is just the beginning; you unlocked a powerful force, and it will help you in future fights. But you won just one battle, not the war …"

"War?" Chin asked nervously.

"Yes, master. Go back and you will find all the answers, as well as new questions, I'm sure."

Chin grabbed the tablet and his backpack, hung the bow and the empty quiver around his neck, and walked back to the old marina. On his way, he saw the three girls running toward him.

"Did you see that, Chin?" asked Acire. "It was awesome! Somebody was lighting up some cool fireworks behind the bushes!"

"Really? Hmm, I must've missed it," Chin said awkwardly.

"Woof, woof!" barked Eagle, running in circles and waving his tail to get some attention and petting from the girls.

"It was great, too bad you missed it," Acire continued, petting Eagle. "Hey, little doggy, why do you have silver paint on your right paw? Did you play with paint?"

"Silver paint?" asked Chin. "Let me see."

"Yeah, and you've also got some silver paint on your neck" said Acire, touching Chin's neck below the silver line.

Chin looked at Eagle's paw that was indeed silver; he touched his neck where Acire was touching him. He felt a long, thin scar, going from his neck and under his jaw in an arc up to his right ear.

Chin remembered the fight and how they had been struck by the explosion after the seventh arrow hit the shadow minion twice. Chin thought about that while touching his new scar. Haras's voice brought him back to the conversation.

"Hey, Chin, do you think I should go on the camping trip?" she asked. "I was afraid of my food allergies, but suddenly I feel like everything will be fine. I don't know why, but I think Mrs. Sallice will be able to take good care of my needs and that I'll just be happy hanging out with the class."

Acire and the other girls looked at each other, puzzled by Haras's words. She had been so negative about the trip just ten minutes earlier. But they smiled, pleased at her change in attitude.

"Of course everything will be perfect," said Acire. "We need to start planning about packing the essential things like hair dryer, matching clothing, organic shampoo and body lotion ..." and they bid farewell to Chin.

Chin smiled and waved back to the girls, happy to see his friend having a positive attitude. He was also thankful he was not a girl!

"Hair dryer? Matching clothing? Body lotion?" whispered Chin to Eagle. "I'm not even sure if I'll take a shower at all during the camping trip ..." And after a small pause, he added "Girls!"

On their way back to the marina, Chin and Eagle saw no shadow minions around the kids. Ekim was still fishing, and it was still quite a challenge to get fish out of Lake Washington. But Ekim was having fun, talking to more experienced fishermen, getting good tips, and trying new bait. Eventually he caught a beautiful silver fish from the blue waters, but he returned it to the lake, feeling it deserved to live as much as people did.

Every kid Chin and Eagle encountered on their way back was as happy as Ekim was—enjoying the moment, trying their best, accomplishing new things by having a positive attitude, and all no longer under the influence of the shadow minion's spell.

"Hmm, there's something I don't quite get yet," said Chin. "Do you see any shadow minions?"

"Yes, but only with the adults, not the kids anymore," replied Eagle.

"Do you think we forgot to do something? I mean the bald eagle told us to go back, and we saw the shadow minion disappearing in a white thunder, but—"

"Let's go back to the secret hall and back home," Eagle said interrupting Chin. "I'm hungry and I need to eat, poop, and rest for a few hours. When I lived in London, we had strict rules about working, eating, and resting ..."

"Yes, Eagle," said Chin, rolling his eyes. "London was so awesome—I know!"

The marina was close by. The fresh smell of water filled the air, and Chin and Eagle hurried to reach the lonely central column as it started to ring.

One, two, three … eight, nine …

"Nine rings? Is it still 9 a.m.?" asked Chin, mystified.

"I don't know what that bell says, but I'm for sure hungry and tired," Eagle complained. "I want to go back home, have supper, and sleep for three days!"

Chin unlocked the magic stone from the bow and put it in place at the end of the shadow cast by the column. In a few seconds, the magic door opened in the same crumbling and dusty way it had closed behind their backs when they had entered a few minutes, hours, or seconds ago. They were not sure anymore about how time was changing in that magical dimension.

Chapter 13

A Reward and Some Answers

After the door opened, Chin and Eagle passed through clouds of dust and small rocks that fell from the stone arch drilled into the giant column.

The heavy door closed behind them with a solid thud. Chin rubbed his eyes, cleaning the dust from his eyelids and trying to get used to the subtle darkness and soft blue glow of the magic hall. Chin noted that the word on the door— *Propositum*—shone with an orange glow.

"Hmm, I wonder what that means," whispered Chin. "We find weird words everywhere: Ab Intra, Propositum—all riddles."

"I agree," Eagle whispered back. "It looks like plain old English isn't enough anymore. Maybe our majesty should do something about it. As soon as I'm back to London for my summer vacation I'll ask her to address this matter properly ..."

As always, Eagle was playful and ready for jokes. As soon as his own eyes got used to the dim light, Eagle ran to the small fountain at the center of the circular hall and got his paws and face wet with the fresh water. In the meantime, Chin put his magic stone back in the box and closed the lid.

"This is the life," Eagle sighed happily. "I love drinking fresh water after a good fight. Just what a guardian dog needs."

"And you deserve it," said the stone guardian suddenly, rocks and dust spewing once more out of his face. "You did an excellent job."

"Well, Chin deserves some credit too," said Eagle. "He was a good helper, but of course we would have been doomed without my unbelievable jump. It was forty feet high!"

"Forty feet? Helper? Here we go again," said Chin with a grin.

"Both of you did an outstanding job. You accomplished your task and vaporized that shadow minion; now the kids of the city are free from the spell of negative thoughts."

"Only the city? That's disappointing," began Chin.

"That's why we have over one hundred guardians in dozens of cities. You just removed the first obstacle here."

"You mean the shadow minion?"

"Yes. That was quite an obstacle. Pure negative thoughts everywhere."

"What happens if a guardian fails in another city?"

"All the cities connect to the final challenge against the Shadow Lord. We can take some losses," said the statue with a sad face.

"I got it. So what happens here now that the shadow minion is gone?"

"Since kids here aren't influenced by negative thoughts anymore, we can reveal to them the secret formulas for getting what they want. That will ultimately help us to win the war over the Shadow Lord."

"What secret formulas? I know nothing about secret formulas. Can you tell me at least one?" asked Chin.

"Which one do you want to know about, master?"

Chin's face lit up with a big smile. He dropped his bow and quiver on the floor, opened his backpack, and took out his black journal and pen. He was ready to take notes on the formulas to later surprise his friends and his parents.

"Can you give me the secret formula for doing homework automatically? Math, language arts, science, everything! I also need the formula for always winning at bowling and getting strikes. Oh yeah, and the formula for eliminating food allergies too so I can help my friend Haras ... and for playing soccer to help my friend Odlanor ... and the formula for not being afraid of the dark ... and the formula to get x-ray vision ... and the one to make myself invisible ..."

Chin went on and on, asking for many more things. He wanted to help himself and his friends. He talked and talked while the guardian said nothing; eventually Chin was silent, waiting for a response.

"This is disappointing, master Chin. Very disappointing. You already have many of those formulas. As a matter of fact, you have one formula that covers most of those requests."

"Really? Which formula?"

"Seahawk will talk to you about that. Now grab your reward from the magic fountain, and do not forget the tablets. You will need them for your next mission."

Chin closed his journal in silence. He was embarrassed for not remembering the secret formula. He looked down and packed his things. Predictably, Eagle was sound asleep by his side, snoring in cadence with the rhythm of the nearby water fountain.

"Don't be sad, master," the guardian said more kindly. "You did an outstanding job, and you deserve some rest and a reward. You are a guardian, and many more adventures await you. Go and get your prize. Go for it! Seahawk will be waiting for you back at home."

The stone guardian then returned to his position, his long spear blocking the tall door, his eyes closed, and his mouth shut. He looked like the other statues again; only the dust and rocks around him indicated that mere seconds ago he was alive and moving. The still-glowing letters at the door were the other indication that something had just happened.

"Eagle, wake up, boy! We have to find our reward!" Chin announced with excitement.

Chin cheered up and walked toward the magic fountain while Eagle was sniffing around trying to help. In the middle of the fountain, close to the center column and in the same place he had found his magic box he saw a shiny orange stone.

Chin picked it up. It was warm and made a rhythmical beat: one, two-three, four … one, two … silence … one, two-three, four … repeating again and again.

Eagle decided to explore the area and went behind some tall rocks, a few yards to the left of the fountain and beyond the six tall columns. Distracted by the beat of the new rock, Chin didn't notice Eagle disappear behind those rocks.

Suddenly a noise cracked the silence, sounding like a thousand rocks crashing to the ground at once. Chin felt the floor shaking and saw a huge cloud of dust billow up behind the six columns, in the same direction that Eagle had gone exploring moments before.

"Eagle, are you okay? Where are you?" shouted Chin, running in the direction of the huge crash.

"Right here, Chin! I need a little help here," Eagle called.

Chin ran fast through the tall second column, through the big rocks that blocked his way after the avalanche, running as fast as he could, guided by Eagle's voice. After a dozen or so yards, he found Eagle covered in dirt from head to tail, clutching a bone-shaped stone in his mouth.

"What happened back here?" Chin asked in shock.

"Uh …" Eagle dropped the stone to speak. "I found this nice bone inside a crack in the wall, and I thought it was a nice one for my personal collection," Eagle answered sheepishly. "But it looks like it was holding everything else in place."

"What a mess!" Chin replied in exasperation. "Can't you stay still for one minute? I thought you learned that at your London school." But Chin was relieved at finding his friend safe among the rocks.

"How did you do that?" asked Eagle.

"Do what?"

"Walk through the columns and through the rocks," Eagle answered in awe. "I think that's marvelous, and I want to learn how to do it. It can be good for finding the bones that all the dogs in the neighborhood hide underground …"

In shock, Chin realized he *had* walked through solid walls made out of stone.

"I guess it's the new magic stone, Eagle—this is the best reward ever!"

Chin and Eagle walked out of the maze of debris, and once they were back in the circular hall, Chin held the stone and ran toward the second column. But a few feet away from it, his doubts assaulted him again, making him slow down. When he finally reached it, he extended his hand, touching the wall's surface. It was as solid as ever.

Puzzled, he tried one more time to go through it, knocking on the wall with a closed fist—still solid. He closed his hand, feeling again the beat of the orange stone. After a few moments, he tried again.

This time his whole hand and arm went all the way through the wall, making him lose his balance and fall forward. He stood up, cleaning the dust from his clothes and realized he was now on the other side of the solid wall.

He sat down on the floor and looked at the giant column guarded by the statue with his spear. It was very solid, as solid as ever. He scratched the surface of the wall with his finger. It was stone.

When he was ready to touch the wall again, he saw Eagle emerging from it, smiling and wagging his tail.

"Thank you for teaching me that!" Eagle announced. "I'll now have the biggest bone collection in our neighborhood!"

"But I didn't teach you anything Eagle!" Chin protested.

"You did a superb job, Chin—now let's go back home. I'm starving, and it's suppertime."

"Yes, let's go back home. Maybe Seahawk can explain things for us."

Still puzzled, Chin put his new orange rock in the front pocket of his pants and walked back through the long hallway, soon emerging from the magic hall.

CHAPTER 14 ─────

Answers and a New Challenge

SEVEN ... EIGHT ... NINE ... Chin and Eagle went through the magic door and found themselves back at the marina in Kirkland. Chin knew he was at the right place when he saw the six columns of the carillon. They could not see any shadow minions around either, and that meant they were back in the real world. It was still nine o'clock in the morning and still raining and windy.

"This time thing is very strange; I don't get it," Chin pondered. "We went down there, did all that stuff and fought the shadow minion, came back, and it's still nine o'clock."

"I don't understand it either, but I'm sure that my sophisticated British stomach knows when it's time for supper. I'm hungry, no matter what time this old clock says."

Chin looked at the dock. Everything was in place: his friend Ekim fishing, the boats, and the people at the coffee shop. The only difference was that in this real world, he could no longer hear other kids' thoughts.

He wanted to talk to Super Abuelo, but he saw no signs of seagulls around. So he decided to walk back to his house. His house wasn't far away, but the spring shower made it seem farther than usual.

"Boy, I'm going to smell like old rubbish when we get back home," said Eagle. "Can you hide me? The last thing I want now is your mom giving me a bath."

"I'm not sure I can help much," Chin replied. "I'll smell like rotten trash too. I guess we'll both be forced to have baths."

"I don't really mind taking a bath," Eagle continued. "I just don't want to remove this beautiful silver color from my right paw. It looks like a royal boot!"

"Wait, Eagle, there's no more silver color on your paw. Can you see the silver scar on my neck? Look here—right under my ear," prompted Chin.

"Nothing, you have no scar," Eagle replied.

Chin stopped and stuck his hand into the front pocket of his pants. The orange stone was still there. He pulled it out of his pocket and opened his hand to look at the soft glow.

"At least the new stone is here, and my quiver is empty, so we know some things are real. Let's move on and get home."

Back at the house, they grabbed a quick snack from the pantry and sneaked out to the backyard where Seahawk was waiting for them, resting on top of the Japanese maple tree.

"Congratulations and welcome back!" said Seahawk. "You two did a fantastic job!"

"Thank you! But we have lot of questions, and you have to tell me all the secret formulas—" Chin began urgently.

"First you have to show me the new stone," interrupted Seahawk.

"Sure! Take a look," said Chin, placing the stone on the ground.

Seahawk jumped from the Japanese maple tree and after an elegant loop went though the branches of the maple tree, through the solid wood columns that supported the deck in Chin's backyard and through the big trunk of the old pine tree. After that impressive flight, he landed softly on top of the magic stone.

"Don't you just love doing that?" asked Seahawk.

"Yes, but how do you do that? I did something similar down there at the magic hall, but when I tried to repeat it, I couldn't do it at first," Chin replied.

"This is only your second magic stone, kid," Seahawk reassured. "To use it you have to believe in yourself and have no doubts. You will get seven more to complete your collection of nine stones. You'll also have magic artifacts like your bow and arrows. With the stones and the artifacts, you'll fight the other five creepy commanders that help the Shadow Lord."

"And how do I do that?" Chin asked hesitantly.

"That is for you to find out. But now that the Propositum door is unlocked and the shadow minion of doubt has disappeared, I think you and many other children won't have such a hard time making magic happen."

Seahawk talked for a long time, answering all the questions that Chin and Eagle had. Chin thought about not having more problems and just making things happen, like when he vaporized the perfect square in the middle of that cloud or when he got the bow and arrows or the compass that he needed.

Or how Odlanor was able to kick that ball at the soccer game or Ekim was fishing at the pier or Haras suddenly thinking she could do just fine at the camp even with her food allergies. Everything made more sense now.

With the shadow minion gone, children had gotten the magic formula to get some of the good experiences they wanted to happen.

"I have to leave now, but remember to go back to the marina next Saturday at nine o'clock. Bring your magic box, both stones, your bow, your golden arrows, and the nine-tails whip. Ab Intra." And Seahawk flew through the walls and over the roof of Chin's house.

"Wait! I don't have any golden arrows!" Chin called to Seahawk's circling form. "I don't even have more silver ones. And what do you mean by nine tails? What's that? Where do I get those?"

"Find those … you have until next Saturday," Seahawk called down.

"Where do I find them? And what does Ab Intra mean?" Chin asked.

"You'll find them. Trust yourself. And check your Latin dictionary—it might come in handy." And old Seahawk disappeared between the clouds.

Chin opened the magic box to take a look at his blue stone, and he noticed a new shape carved on the inside of the box. It was a perfect fit for his new orange stone.

He put his new stone inside that new niche, and the words *Ab Intra* glowed in alternated colors: orange, blue, orange, repeating the same pattern again and again.

CHAPTER 15 ——————

Testing New Powers and Finding a Precious Meaning

THAT AFTERNOON, CHIN WENT TO THE Kirkland library to check out some good adventure books. After his own real-life adventure, he was ready for a break. Since he had a few days before the new challenge, he decided that reading a good book would be the best reward. The library was not far from his house, and after the morning rain, the sky was clear and sunny, perfect for a walk.

On his way there, with Eagle trotting happily at his side, he thought about the mission he had accomplished and about the words from old Seahawk. He kept looking around for shadow minions, but he could not find even one. He was still confused by his recent experience.

Walking down Central Way Avenue, he saw the big local baseball field at Peter Kirk Park. The baseball season had started, and kids from Little League were warming up. Chin smiled after confirming that not a single shadow minion was bothering the kids. He thought it was going to be a great game with kids playing without fear of failure.

Once he turned the corner of Central Way and Third Avenue, he came upon the public parking building and behind that the public library.

"Too bad I didn't bring my orange stone, Eagle," Chin said. "We could go right through the wall and save some time!"

"We still can do it. Once you put the stone inside the magic box, you get the powers with you—even if you're not holding the stone, remember?" Eagle said. "After all, you can talk Doggy with me, and you don't have the blue stone with you."

"I do *not* speak Doggy!" Chin protested. "But wait a second, you're right about going through the wall, Eagle! Let's try with that tree."

Chin pointed toward a maple tree planted in the picnic area to the west side of the baseball field. It was a medium-sized tree with a fairly narrow trunk. Yet for Chin it was as solid as the concrete columns supporting the parking lot building.

"Looks like somebody isn't sure about his powers," said Eagle. "Let's go all the way through the walls! But we can start with that little tree. As a trained officer of London's Scotland Yard police, I am not afraid of big challenges!"

"Are you going to keep bugging me with that Scotland Yard story you made up?" Chin asked.

Eagle didn't listen and ran fast in the direction of the tree; without hesitation he went through the solid wood and quickly appeared on the other side.

"That was really easy! Now let me pee here so we can mark this tree as my first successful experience going through things in the real world," Eagle said triumphantly.

Chin was speechless, standing still twenty feet from the tree. He focused on the task and with new resolution walked toward the tree.

With his arms and hands extended in front of him, he yelled, "I can do it, I can do it, I can do it!"

His hands and arms went all the way through the dense wood, but then he hesitated. At that moment, the wood turned solid again, and he bounced back, falling on the soft grass.

"You need more training, but you will do it soon for sure," Eagle reassured him. "Why don't you pee and mark the tree too? That always helps!"

Chin was silent, half disappointed, half encouraged by the way he had almost made it.

"I can do it; I know I'll do it," Chin finally said. "Today we'll take the long way around the building. I'll be ready soon."

Before entering the library, Chin left Eagle with his good friend Bob. Bob owned a café across the street and was very good with dogs.

Most of the patrons going to the library left their dogs with Bob. He took care of the animals with much love. It was good for his business too, since most people had a coffee, a cup of tea, or a delicious piece of chocolate cake when leaving or picking up their pets.

Inside the library, Chin walked to the children's section to check out a new adventure book. He saw a big dictionary opened on a small podium, right by the librarian's desk. He observed that dictionary every time he was there but had never thought about using it. After all, it was much easier to search for things on the Internet. He stopped for a moment and stared at the big old dictionary.

"Do you need help?" asked the librarian. She smiled encouragingly at Chin.

"No, thank you. Well, maybe I do. Do you know if that dictionary has words in Latin?" Chin asked shyly.

"What are you looking for?" the librarian asked gently.

"It's a phrase I heard, but I don't know what it means: Ab Intra," said Chin, showing the librarian the phrase written in his black journal.

"Hmm, it sounds familiar, and I know exactly what you need."

The librarian typed some words on her computer and after a few seconds wrote something on a piece of paper.

"Here you have it—check out this book. I'm sure you'll find the answer there."

Chin took the piece of paper and read it: "Latin-English dictionary, book number 22784532, section REF 473.21." His heart was pounding faster and faster. He thought about the encryption in his magic box and the magic tablets and the bald eagle helping him to focus on the battle with the shadow minion. The words *Ab Intra* were always present.

He walked through the hallways and checked many bookcases until he found it. He also found another book on that shelf: "Dictionary of Latin Quotations, 2044179378, Redmond Library." Chin thought it was odd to find a book from a different library on that shelf.

He grabbed both books, and barely containing his excitement, he ran to the nearest table and opened the first book. He found the meaning for "ab" on the first page and the meaning for "intra" on page 323, but it was still confusing.

He looked at the book of quotations and after a few minutes he found it: Ab Intra. He read the section many times with a smile on his face.

Now it makes total sense! he thought.

"I got it," he whispered. "I got it!" he repeated louder. "I got it!" he said again, now almost yelling and forgetting he was at the library.

He opened his black journal and wrote with fast strokes the definition he had found. He added some personal notes, and then he left both books open on the table.

Chin totally forgot about the adventure book he had wanted to check out and ran outside to meet Eagle. He could scarcely believe it—he had solved the mysterious encryption.

"I got it, Eagle! I found out what Ab Intra means," said Chin, holding his black journal up. "And I wrote it all here so we don't ever forget it!"

"It's about time," Eagle replied. "I remember my Latin classes back in London. I was always the best dog in the class because I barked in Latin in a very clear, crisp tone. It wasn't easy but a good Italian dog taught me the proper accent."

"Wait a minute, Eagle—you knew what *Ab Intra* meant all the time?"

"Of course!" Eagle replied calmly. "How do you think I jumped forty feet to help you battle the shadow minion? Or how could I get through the trees using the secret power of the orange stone?"

"And why did you never tell me?" Chin protested.

"Oh well, you never asked me in a proper way, my lord. And besides, I thought you knew it deep down inside, even though you didn't realize you knew it. Everything comes from inside. We must believe in ourselves, and the right things will happen, magical or not. Super Abuelo was right! What *do* they teach at school these days?"

"Latin is boring! Why would they teach us that in fifth grade?" Chin asked.

"It's not boring at all. But wait, it's almost suppertime; we should go back because I'm hungry," concluded Eagle.

"Yes, you're always hungry!" Chin laughed.

And without further delay, Chin and Eagle walked back home.

CHAPTER 16 ———————

A Surprise and a New Challenge

BACK AT HOME, CHIN WAS HAPPY to see his dad's car parked in the garage. He looked at the car's charge-gauge and it was at 100 percent, which meant his dad had been in the house for at least twenty minutes.

He took Eagle's plate and served him a cup of organic dog food, topping the plate with two pieces of carrot as special treats.

"Here you have it, boy, dinner is ready for you," Chin announced.

"Thank you, I was fainting from hunger," Eagle said with his usual exaggeration. "Supper is just what I needed."

Chin ran to greet his father.

"Hi, Dad!"

"Hi, Chin—I have two small surprises for you. Forrest sent you a package, and I rented a house at the beach for our summer vacation—we're going to San Luis Obispo. We'll spend four weeks there, and Eagle can come with us."

"Wow, that's super," Chin replied in surprise. "When do we leave, Dad?"

"Right after you finish school, the third week of June."

"Great! Where's the package from Forrest?"

"It's upstairs—I put it on your desk. It's a long, narrow package, but not very heavy. I wonder if it's another bow or more arrows."

"Maybe—I'll take a look at it," Chin replied with excitement.

Chin called Eagle and quickly ran upstairs. He put his black journal on his desk and grabbed his pocketknife to carefully open the package from Forrest. Inside the package, he found two long pieces wrapped in newspaper pages for additional protection.

He unwrapped the first piece and found a golden arrow; it was three feet long and made from some sort of yellow crystal. The point was a dark, sharp stone, and the tail was adorned with five feathers from different birds. He could recognize the black feather from a big crow or a raven, the white feather from the tail of a bald eagle, and the peacock feather, which was longer that the other ones, with many different colors and a beautiful design in the shape of an eye. But he couldn't recognize the other two feathers. Another was shorter than the others and was deep green, and the fifth one was red and black.

He put the arrow aside and took the other object. After unwrapping it, he found a sleek bunch of black and light brown leather intertwined. It was a beautiful whip, and he observed that the base of the handle was made from the same red wood of his bow—the red wood from the magic cave in Sedona, Arizona.

"One, two, three, four, five, six, seven, eight, nine ... nine tails! Just what I needed!" Chin exclaimed. "And a brand new golden arrow!"

"You're getting better and better at visualizing things," said Eagle. "It took you two days to get the magic blue box for your stone, but this time it was only a few hours after Seahawk told you about the nine tails and the arrow!"

"Yes," murmured Chin, thinking about what Eagle had said. He knew that just wishing for something wasn't enough to make it happen, but he wondered more and more if visualizing things that he wanted in life could change his actions and make him be more persistent in going out and getting what he wanted, or if indeed something magical was happening.

Chin examined the whip carefully; it was a beautiful work of art from his friend Forrest. He noted a small carving at the base of the whip, right on the red wood.

"Do you see this, Eagle? Does it look familiar to you?"

"Indeed, master—it is a perfect niche on that handle, excellent for hiding some treats and having some food handy."

"No, Eagle," Chin said patiently. "I think it's a perfect fit for something else."

Chin opened his magic box and took out the orange stone. He placed the stone at the base of the whip. Once again it was a perfect fit, and with a firm pressure from his hand, the stone locked in place with a solid clicking sound. The whole whip glowed with a soft orange light, and an encryption surfaced from the red wood: Ab Intra.

Before tossing out the box, Chin checked the interior one more time. At the bottom he found a handwritten note from his friend Forrest.

It was a story written with black and orange ink, with some letters in orange, some letters in black, arranged in such a way that from a distance it looked like a drawing of a coyote at the border of a cliff.

After reading a few lines, Chin recognized the story; it was an old tale from the Native Americans of the Pacific Northwest. Forrest had shared the story with him when Chin was in Arizona the previous fall.

It was about *Wishy*—a coyote who was never content with what he was and was always trying to be something else: a raccoon, a bear, a salmon, a bald eagle ... and how after falling down from a big cliff while pretending to be an eagle, his fur got stuck in the branches of the trees, forming a moss that grows in the northwest forests and that is known as *Cojo fur.*

The moral of the story was to never try to be better than somebody or something else, just to be oneself.

Chin could not understand how the story was related to the whip and the arrow or with his appointment as a guardian, and it was strange that his friend did not include anything else—just the ancient tale.

Once he read the story for the third time, he noticed an odd trace on the paper surrounding Forrest's signature. He smiled and took the orange stone from the whip and put it on the paper, inside the odd drawing—it was a perfect match!

As soon as Chin did that, the paper turned orange, making all the orange letters disappear. He thought at first it was just a nice trick, but after a few moments, he saw something else.

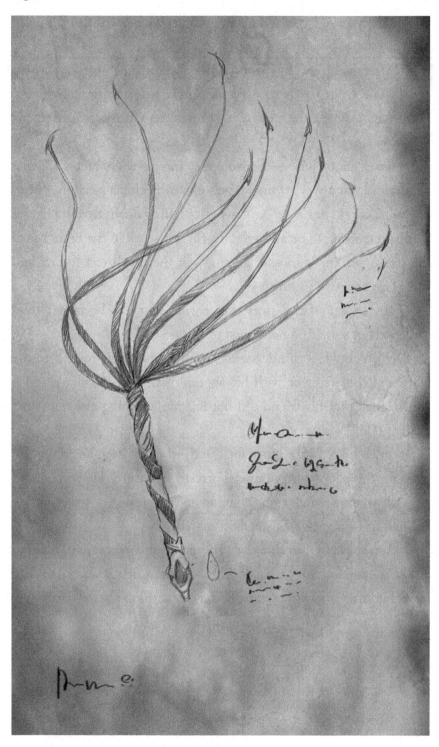

"Eagle, look at this! If I put together only the black letters, I can read new words. The first words are: *You are in great danger, and we must change plans ...*"

Chin grabbed his black journal and started to arrange letters, forming the right words.

Everything changed! What looked like an innocent tale for kids became an urgent call from his friend, the master chief, describing last-minute changes to the plan that Seahawk had discussed with him hours earlier.

The Shadow Lord had blocked the entrance to the magic hall at the old marina in Kirkland; Chin would need to enter through the back door in the Central California Coast.

It was a secret message from Forrest, with precise instructions on how to open the back door using his blue magic stone and asking him to bring the bow, the golden arrow, and the nine-tails whip. One of the Shadow Lord commanders, *Lavahydra*, was working with the Shadow Lord on a comeback with a powerful secret weapon.

Chin was excited by the new challenge but was still unclear on the location of the back door. California was a very big state, and the coast was hundreds of miles long.

The message from Forrest ended with the following description, next to a map of a circular hall and six doors:

On the bishop's land
The secret door waits
Where the bear feeds from figs
Where the water meets the third cut into a rich hill
When the ninth bell rings
The guardian uses the key

Chin was sure that the riddle was a clear direction to find the back door entrance to the magic hall. He read it aloud many times until he had memorized it.

"This is a hard one, Eagle. I need more clues—the California coast is huge," said Chin, while tracing with his finger the border of the California coast on the map hanging on his wall. "There are too many places; I don't know where to start."

"Maybe you should start at the center; you said it was the central coast," Eagle suggested.

"Yes, but the center is still big: San Francisco, Santa Cruz, Salinas, Santa Maria, Santa Barbara. It looks like a lot of saints, but no bishops!"

"Any other names on the map?" Eagle asked.

"Yes, many others, but no bishops. Just more names of saints: San Luis Obispo, San Jose …"

"You found it!" Eagle said excitedly.

"Where? What do you mean?" Chin asked.

"What do you learn at school? I thought you had Spanish classes—furthermore you're fully bilingual!" Eagle insisted.

"Yes, I am, but I still don't get it," Chin insisted.

"Obispo means Bishop … in Spanish," Eagle announced.

"San Luis Obispo, of course, that's the place," Chin almost crowed. "So I guess it's not by chance that my dad rented a house for our vacation there."

"Well, it looks like nothing happens by chance nowadays, my lord," Eagle teased.

Chin grabbed his pen and took some more notes in his black journal. When finished, he placed the orange stone back inside his magic box. He was ready for the next adventure!

*   *   *

Over one thousand miles away, in a small city on the California coast, an unusually warm and dense fog covered Pismo Beach and Los Osos, climbing the mountains, seeping under doors and windows until it filled every single house, every building, and every park in San Luis Obispo. The fog moved fast, with a sinister sound.

Frrr, flrrr, frrr, flrrr ...

Underground, more than four hundred feet deep, the nine heads of the Lavahydra opened their mouths, pouring the dense fog that through secret tunnels surfaced in San Luis Obispo, Cayucos, Los Osos, Atascadero, Pismo Beach, and the whole vicinity.

Back in Kirkland, Chin saw Eagle's right paw turning silver and the orange and blue light coming out of the magic box filling his room.

On top of Chin's desk, the black journal lay open, and the rays coming out of the magic box illuminated four words. It was the note that Chin took in a hurry at the library after finding the answer in the old book that the librarian pointed him to:

Ab Intra: From within.

•••••••••••••••••••••••